If it is your life

By the same author from Penguin Books

You Have to be Careful in the Land of the Free
Where I Was
Kieron Smith, boy

If it is your life

JAMES KELMAN

HAMISH HAMILTON
an imprint of
PENGUIN BOOKS

HAMISH HAMILTON

Published by the Penguin Group
Penguin Books Ltd, 80 Strand, London WC2R ORL, England
Penguin Group (USA) Inc., 375 Hudson Street, New York, New York 10014, USA
Penguin Group (Canada), 90 Eglinton Avenue East, Suite 700, Toronto, Ontario, Canada M4P 2Y3
(a division of Pearson Penguin Canada Inc.)
Penguin Ireland, 25 St Stephen's Green, Dublin 2, Ireland (a division of Penguin Books Ltd)
Penguin Group (Australia), 250 Camberwell Road,
Camberwell, Victoria 3124, Australia (a division of Pearson Australia Group Pty Ltd)
Penguin Books India Pvt Ltd, 11 Community Centre,
Panchsheel Park, New Delhi – 110 017, India
Penguin Group (NZ), 67 Apollo Drive, Rosedale, North Shore 0632, New Zealand
(a division of Pearson New Zealand Ltd)
Penguin Books (South Africa) (Pty) Ltd, 24 Sturdee Avenue,
Rosebank, Johannesburg 2196,
South Africa

Penguin Books Ltd, Registered Offices: 80 Strand, London WC2R ORL, England

www.penguin.com

First published 2010
1

Set in 13/15.75 pt Monotype Dante
Typeset by MPS Limited, A Macmillan Company
Printed in Great Britain by Clays Ltd, St Ives plc

A CIP catalogue record for this book is available from the British Library

ISBN: 978-0-241-14242-4

Contents

Acknowledgements

'Tricky times ahead pal' previously published in *Breathing Space/The Herald*, 2010; 'Ingrained' previously published in *Five Dials*, 2009; 'talking about my wife' previously published in *Headshook*, 2009; 'justice for one' previously published in *The Stinging Fly*, Dublin 2009; 'The Gate' previously published in *The Herald*, 2008; 'Man to Man' previously published in *In Pubs* by Stuart Murray, Glasgow 2006; 'The Later Transgression' previously published in *Flash*, University of Chester 2008; 'Vacuum' previously published in *Edinburgh Review*, 2009: an earlier version of 'Pieces of shit do not have the power to speak' (entitled 'In the dungeon') previously published in *Starting at Zero*, Etruscan Books, South Devon 2006.

Tricky times ahead pal

When I presented myself at the Emergency section of the Social Security Office I knew things could go wrong but I was not expecting a leg amputated. But that was the situation. I would have expected an alternative but there was none. This was clear to anybody who knows anything about anything. Not just about the British welfare system, nor indeed state-run hospitals. Nor legs for that matter, at the risk of sounding facetious. This is what they gave me to understand.

Neither was it a situation facing me. They made that clear. It was a situation in itself. It would have faced anybody who was human. If you were not human then no, obviously. Most entities who walked were human but there are other possible worlds and I would never discount them, nor intelligences within.

Furthermore, it was my own negligence concerning the cause; secondly the effect; thirdly the relation between the two. This required not only a basic grasp of atomic theory but the results thereon of the faculty of common sense and that relation. But what docs that mean, that last statement, its apparent meaninglessness.

At that time I did not grasp the significance of my bodily functioning and the changes then taking place. A logic was in operation. At least I grasped that, and

my culpability. I was not one to fool myself. I simply
had not realized what was happening. Had it been some
other body I would have, especially that of an acquaintance. One's perception alters when it is you yourself.

Before the amputation they once again advised me
of its necessity. I had a sudden horror flash about those
poor creatures who have a fetish about amputation; left
to their own devices they would have every limb on
their body chopped asunder. Let them be under no illu-
sions! Only if it is absolutely essential, I said.

Beyond all shadow of a doubt, commented someone
in regard to the medical findings.

I thought it in bad taste. The comment may have
occurred while I was under anaesthetic. I accepted its
truth eventually. It depressed the very air in my body. A
mist descended behind my eyes, entering my mind,
seeping its way into what remained of my brains. This
was after the operation. I was removed to the Homeless Recovery Unit which was located in the very bowels
of the earth. To the embarrassment of the staff responsible for administering the anaesthetics I clung onto my
dreams. One concerned the possibility of one-legged
midfielders playing in a World Cup. Would I ever play
football again!

How embarrassing. Can we even describe such nonsense as thought? I had not played a game for ten years
so who was I kidding.

But can a man not dream?

No, not in this manner. I was referred to Counsel-
ling. It then transpired that in the darker recesses of my

inner being and prior to the amputation I assumed I might still play for my country. Certainly in international matches. This though I had never played professional football at any time, not having progressed beyond the lower divisions of the outermost community leagues. Our womenfolk paid money that we men might play. In those far-off days I was a family man and expected such money to be skimmed off the housekeeping.

Down in the Recovery Unit I lost and found consciousness, a veil ascending, a human shape by the foot of the bed was passing through and I called: Is it true that one-legged midfield players will not be selected for national honours?

Once I had recovered enough to crawl about, a couple of welfare orderlies assisted me upwards, and a belated return to the Emergency section. The Homeless Physiotherapy Unit lay three corridors distant. I spent a while here. Sad to relate, as will have become apparent, I had nowhere to hop, one's long-term relationship having failed four years and three months previously. I could pinpoint the time to the day. There is nought surprising about that, rather the reverse, as clever rhetoricians would argue.

I do not know what legs might have to do with that. I do not care about legs, about my legs. Not then, not now. Never. I do not care.

Lump it.

I had given up alcohol prior to this low point in my life which, according to Form 12/7bd, was Week 3 Post-op.

It seemed longer but that was normal, due partly to the medication. I was fit enough to deal with the paperwork. If not the Reception Clerk was there to help. The condition I was in helped matters but not sufficiently, I still had to deal with it. The Reception Clerk was pleasant and humane. At first I enjoyed her femininity. I have to say that. I want to be clear and honest. These are significant matters, empirical matters.

She helped me fill in the forms then faxed copies to Personnel for corroboration. At this juncture our relationship soured. I asked why everything must go through Personnel? I said: Surely if we are dealing with Social Security then Personnel does not enter the equation. Let us posit analogies; one thinks of the Social Security department of Great Britain as the political arm of a fascist state; does one therefore consider the Personnel section of said department as the Gestapo?

Contrary to what the Reception Clerk believed I was not taking this at or on a personal level. I did not feel in any way compromised. But I was angry and confess that I was. I had been divested of a damn leg, I said, in circumstances that are less than transparent.

Oh but that is how it is, she said. She smiled a smile that progressed beyond the merely polite. Affairs are more difficult for us.

I frowned, for this was a surprising gesture of solidarity. The woman gazed sideways. I thought Personnel had become a euphemism, I said.

Fortunately she pretended not to have heard and called over a young chap. She asked him to visit the local Oxfam shop on my behalf. I sat on a bench to wait. He soon returned with a pair of trousers. The woman produced scissors, snipped off one leg and passed me the needle and thread with which one might sew up the loose end.

The cost of the purchase was deducted from next week's allowance. I borrowed the key to the toilet, leaving a £5 deposit for its safe return. I hopped along to try on the breeks. Inside a cubicle I held them up for inspection. Obviously the young chap had treated my future with impunity. These breeks must have been far too large, far too large, this leg was like – fuck sake man it was like a fucking pillow case. But better that than the other way, too small or something, tight and just

I pulled it on. Oh my Jesus Christ almighty it was the left leg the woman had snipped off. Oh man I was toppling, flapped my hands at the wall, steadied myself.

Why had she not allowed me to do it myself! Obviously it was the right leg that required the amputation. She had watched me approach her damn desk. So now I had to wear the trouser back to front.

The pain was excruciating; I was biting my lip, brow pressed against my wrist, propped against the wall, eyes closed. Its intensity subsided, passed. I reached round to close up the top of the garment which was now round at my arse but it was too difficult. There was a mirror but it was too high up the wall and of no assistance unless if I sat up on the washhand basin. If I did my rear-end would be hidden. I would be unable to reach round myself given I was thin. I used to be thickset. I still – could – not – reach – round. I could not. So aggravating, just damn bloody aggravating. I twisted and turned. I bit into my lower lip again and made further stabs at it. Try as I might I just could not fasten the garment.

Fortunate was I that the pain ceased. By now the good leg was numb. I call it the good leg, of course it was the only one. I hopped back out, clinging onto the ends of the trousers, hopping to the rear of the queue.

I was thinking of one good leg and one bad leg, the good being the whole and the bad being the stump. This was a defence mechanism of the emotions.

When I reached the Emergency desk it was to find another receptionist on duty. A woman of about thirty-six years of age. She had that maturity, allied to youth, allied to blouse; women wear such blouses, I heard of a fellow whose nose dropped down a cleavage. She looked at me. I explained that which had transpired. She was attentive, noted all the details, which she emailed immediately to Personnel. She keyed in additional data and that was that, my presence, its necessity.

Along the way to the exit an old guy was guarding a space by a radiator. He wore an eye-patch and had a bandage wrapped round his head; a twisted bandage, it must have been uncomfortable. Judging by the lack of a bump on the left side of his head he was missing an ear. That may have explained why his posture was so curious. He was somehow not even standing, not what you would call standing. He rocked on the very rearmost edge of his heels though he seemed asleep. But he was not asleep. He was heating his hands.

He looked at me, noting the problem I had with the back-to-front one-legged garment. How would he have described me? The one-legged bloke with the back-to-front trouser(s).

Behind us was the queue of people at Emergency reception. The old guy seemed to be wondering what explanation existed for my present state. There was none, it was just the way of the world. He hesitated, adjusted the bandage about his head. When I passed him by he called after me: Heh pal!

Yeh? I hopped a step sideways to look behind.

Will I zip up yer trousers at the back?

That would be good, I said, thanks, thanks a lot.

Saves a wee bit of embarrassment, he added.

Definitely. I balanced myself against the wall. When the zip was applied I could relax, and I did relax, just that little bit; that little bit was not only necessary it was enough. I flexed my wrist muscles.

Okay? said the old guy.

Yeh.

But when I went to put my hands in my pockets it was so very awkward, very very awkward, just about damn impossible.

What's up? he said.

Aw nothing. Just life, always something.

Dont I know it!

Thanks anyway.

Take it easy pal. Tricky times ahead.

You're right, I said.

He was, he was spot on. The experience of age. Suddenly I remembered the £5 deposit on the key to the toilet but I had left the damn thing in the doorlock. It would have vanished by now. There was a café I knew where £5 bought you a cup of tea and a baked potato. The same £5 got you two cups of tea and a sandwich. That was what ye got for yer £5. Not bad really, although it was not so much a café as a snackbar, located at a supermarket entrance. This entrance was also the exit and folks like me, well, anyway, I did go along on occasion. The Security man was always a snag. If he was there individuals had to dodge through.

That was the supermarket this was the Social Security. It too had an exit and I was interested to see it. In the old days I named it 'the escape hatch'. My heart leapt when I spied it. In future times, whenever I returned here, and was obliged to leave, I would view it differently. But I should have told the old guy about the £5 deposit, he could have taken a chance on the key, but no he wouldnt, he wouldnt, an old fellow like that; to some he was a hero.

Our Times

There was this upper-middle-class guy who was a genuine goody. Charles was his name. He may have been called after the English monarch. I did not know him personally and might have thought highly of him if I had. We shall never know. He was a boring individual in adult company but children suffered him and allowed him to join their games. On the whole his life was boring insofar as anyone's life is boring. But I was serious when I said I regarded him highly.

This will have the mark of authenticity about it.

Charles had a full-time upper-middle-class type of job. At the same time he was a complete individual, a whole human being, figuratively. So too was Sian, his wife. Sian is an unusual name for a woman which was of additional interest to myself, as is the Gaelic tradition.

Charles and Sian shared an interest in the arts and were at ease in their own community. This appealed to me. She was of the middling-middle-class; a girl who, prior to the first pregnancy, held a responsible position in a local law firm. She would pick up her career where she had left off. Once her youngest child reached nursery-school age, she hoped. Sian was counting the months.

Theirs were decent children, neither stuck-up nor namby-pamby. They did not feel ill at ease if adults were in the same room yet had their own little circle of friends. They made no attempt to dominate mixed-age companies. Charles was proud of that. He disliked children being pushed to the fore in adult society. He thought it demeaning.

Sian thought the same but in her it occasioned pangs of guilt. In a curious way she was proud of that guilt. Yet the guilt itself was a secret and she disliked secrets. One night she blurted it out to Charles. His only reply was a smile. Sian liked his smile. It was beautiful. Oddly it was their daughter who inherited the smile. Sian wished it were the boy. Their smile reminded her of her own father and she had never much cared for him, nor his memory.

Twice a year the family holidayed together. These were not unadventurous forays and were thoroughly enjoyed. So much so that Charles and Sian intended selling up and moving abroad to a similar destination if only they could wangle early retirement. Times had become tough but they did stand a chance. I am not sure if ever they did wangle it. We only heard about them from neighbours. Each time I saw these particular neighbours it was not only a reminder but a rejoinder. I was aware of Charles's existence but was fortunate to have an independent circle of friends I could describe as 'mine' rather than 'ours'.

talking about my wife

I should have been working or else calling into the pub for a couple of pints before the last stretch home. I sometimes did that coming off the nightshift on Friday mornings. Even if I was working an overtime shift into Saturday, I still liked that Friday morning. There was a pub near the cross that opened for breakfast. A couple of us went in there. We did not stay long, an hour or so, three or four pints. The lasses were well away to school by the time I strolled home and Cath would be up and about, giving me looks.

Anyway, she had been asleep when I opened the door. So how come I was home like this? I saw the question. She was frowning and blinking at the alarm clock on the dressing table. Dont worry, I said, it's no time to get up yet.

She turned her head from me, her eyes closed. She aye had difficulty getting out of bed. I had difficulty getting in it.

I leaned across to her, laying my hand on her thigh. She screwed up her eyes, gave a slight shudder instead of a smile then her exaggerated shiver; she should have had that copyrighted – or copywritten, whatever you say.

She lay further down, pulling over the quilt and snuggling in. I grinned. She was more awake now, squinting at me which meant I was to speak. Explain yourself man! I might have smiled.

My presence at such an ungodly hour! I could only shrug and tell her the truth, an approximation to the truth. I had a fall-out with the gaffer, there was a bit of bother. Other women might have accepted that. Cath was not other women, and her silence continued. Are you going back to sleep? I said.

She ignored this. What does 'ignored' mean? I do not know. I have to be honest, I was rather weary. I sat down on the bedside chair and unknotted my shoelaces. Oh dear, the shoes. She hated me wearing shoes in the house, especially the bedroom, but anyplace where bare feet were liable to tread. Our lasses had pals and when they brought them into the house they forgot to tell them to take off their shoes. This drove Cath nuts. I did not blame her but it caused emotional mayhem in the highways and byways of our apartment. Then again the lasses did not like telling their pals to take off their shoes. It made them seem stupid, that was what they said. Oh mum nobody else does it.

I dont care what nobody else does.

But they tell people in school and they laugh at us!

I stayed out it. Domestic issues are an awkward reality. Very much so in our house.

What I was thinking was get my own shoes off and a quick wash and into bed. Tomorrow is a brand-new day. Except literally it was not. It was the exact same day as here and now. It was Friday morning and would be Friday dinnertime when I arose Sir Frederick, arise ye and walk the plank ere doom befall ye.

Man, what a life.

She lowered the quilt to beneath her boobs. I was about to say something further but the mammarian physicality beat me. I reached to hold her hand instead. But even that was off-putting. Cath's hand is a really sort of pleasant thing, it is soft and warm. I always found it pleasing in an aesthetic way. I used to like drawing when I was a boy. I would have drawn her hand. Her fingers were long and seemed to taper, and then if she had a varnish on her nails. It just looked good. Had I been that way inclined I would have varnished my nails.

And what do I mean 'that way inclined'! So now when I looked at her, with silly thoughts crossing my mind, I could only smile and this made her suspicious. So how are *you* doing? I said. Did *you* sleep?

She did not answer. I was suddenly tired, most tired, needing to stretch out beside her on the bed here and now, right here and now. I took off my second shoe but continued sitting there. And a song went through my mind. My little nephew sang it to me a week past and it went something like:

> *I'm so silly*
> *silly silly silly.*

Me and him sang it walking up and down the hallway like a pair of demented soldiers:

> *I'm so silly*
> *silly silly silly.*

I would like to have done it with the gaffer. That bastard. I would have goose-stepped him along the factory floor, Groucho Marx and Ginger Rogers:

I'm so silly
silly silly silly.

Aw well. And my neck. Interesting to note that I had developed a nervous condition on the right side of my neck; it entered spasms at the slightest emotional activity in one's brainbox. All soldiers are demented. All professional ones anyway. Everytime I hear one talking I want to have their parents arrested for child abuse. I mean ordinary soldiers, not these upper-class fuckers who march them as to war.

I sighed, I was enjoying the seat. So: this was Cath I was talking to. Well well well.

The truth is me and her were incompatible. On occasion. Was this such an occasion! I guffawed inwardly, and needed to sneeze immediately, grabbed for a tissue from her side of the bed, and gave the snout a hearty blow. I think there is something wrong with my nose, I said.

Oh that is interesting, muttered one's missis.

What is that new-fangled expression, 'pear-shaped'? I think it might describe my life.

So what happens now? she said.

In what respect I thought but said nothing. What happens now? Worth pondering. What does 'what' mean? Even before getting to 'now' that statement was beyond my intellectual capacity. 'Happens' is just a verb, which makes comprehension easy. With verbs concepts are straightforward, it is the actual doing that causes trouble, translating into action, getting from concept to movement.

Man, how many pints did I not have? This is the last time I would forgo my Friday-morning breakfast booze-up.

But I felt like a sandwich, a bit of toast or something.

Cath sighed. I sighed as well. But her sighs were significant. Mine were just sighs.

Fucked again I thought, but in what way? I did not answer the sigh lest incriminated. Except when Cath sighs one is required to answer. What is troubling you madame?

No, I did not say that. I did not, in nowise, say that. Fear. Not in so many words. Nor was I sure what to say. I got up from the chair and walked to the window, parted the curtains a little. Your Honour, I cannot deny that that is what occurred on the morning of the fourteenth.

Maybe she wanted a cup of teh. Her pronunciation of this aye reminded me of her grannie, a lass from Mayo whom I met and loved for one week in the merry month of July, during my courtship of the illustrious Catrine her granddaughter.

I was about to ask if she wanted a cup but she spoke first. Do you mean you have got the sack?

Of course not!

Of course not? Did I actually say that? What a fucking liar man! I would have burst out laughing except she was staring at me, staring me down. I had been about to look out the window. Now I felt like a total tube, like a naughty boy, I said, caught in the act. That is what I feel like.

So what is it? she said. What happened? Was it a fallout? What actually happened? Do you really mean you got the sack?

I smiled. You are some woman, telling you, the way ye say stuff.

So you have not been sacked?

Sacked! Even the word sounds strange to the ear, to my ear anyway. When the hell was I ever sacked? Have I ever been sacked? I cannot remember. I do not think I was ever sacked, not in my whole life.

'Sacked'. There is something anti-human about that term. I do not care for it. Here you are as an adult human being, a thinking being to use the ppolitical terminology, and then you are to be 'sacked', this canvas bag is to be pulled over you, hiding you completely. None can see one. Then one is smuggled publicly from the place of one's employment, in the erstwhile sense.

Sacked, I said, what a word!

Cath looked into my eyes with a steady gaze, her sparkling blue eyes shining as befits a latterday femme fatale, one who is given to ascertaining the thoughts of a mancub by return so to speak; in other words, as soon as one has the thoughts they are transcribed into her nut.

I hope this makes sense, I said, what happened apparently is that I was sacked.

She wanted further information. Her continued silence indicated that. The truth is she was an innocent. There are a lot of women like Cath. They know nothing. Cath knew nothing. She had never experienced the actuality of work. Genuine work. Jobs where things like 'angry gaffer' and 'sack' crop up regularly. In her whole life she had never worked in an ordinary hourly paid job. Office stuff was all she did. That was a thing about women, they were all middle-class. She knew nothing about real life, the kind of job where if ye told a gaffer to eff off you collect yer cards at the end of the week. That was power and that was powerlessness.

Would you like a slice of toast? I said.

She did not answer. Other matters were of moment, weightier than toast.

No they were not. Come on, I said, let us have a bit of toast, a cup of tea.

Cath studied me. This was no time for toast and tea. Life was too important. Seriously, I said, I am not powerless, I have it in me to act and here I am not so much acting as in action, I am making toast and tea.

Cath did not smile. My attitude is more being than assumption of such. She knows this and does not care for it. When we were winching, back in the good old days when choice was probable

I lost that train of thought.

Here is the reality: I was an ordinary worker. Power there is none. It did not matter I was a would-be author on matters cultural, ppolitical and historical, to wit my life. None of that mattered. I existed in the world of 'angry gaffers', data such as 'sack' and other matters of fact.

Man, I was fucking sick of it. And having to please everybody. That was part of it. That was an essential part of it. Then coming home here and having to do the same in one's domestic life. It was so fucking – oh man

Sorry Cath, what did you say? the thought returneth.

I didnt say anything.

I thought you did. Because there is no point attacking me like it is my fault, it is not my fault.

I didnt say anything.

I am glad because really

I did not say anything.

Right.

I am not attacking you.

Okay then but in a sense you are, your manner. It is like you are blaming me. That is like what you are doing. You dont say anything except just look but you do look, you look at me, and it means things that are mentally uncomfortable, psychologically I should say.

I beg your pardon? Cath almost smiled.

You're blaming me without even knowing the circumstances.

I'm not.

I think you are, you have been. I'm sorry, if I jumped the gun, I'm sorry.

Cath sniffed softly, continued to study me. She was no longer lying on her back: I should have pointed this out. By now she had raised herself onto her elbows then plumped up a pillow and squeezed it behind her shoulders, and propped herself against the headboard. She did all of that while I was blethering like a dangblasted nincompoop. Her arms lay in a natural damn position across her lap which lay concealed beneath the quilt. Mind you,

no, forget that.

Cath was entitled to stare at me and stare she did. And I was entitled to ask why. There are no bones to be picked.

What are you talking about?

I shrugged, coughed to clear my throat.

Did he honestly sack you?

No, I said, not at all.

Honestly?

Honestly.

She shook her head. An instant prior to that I realized that my lies were no good: my lies never had been: my lies were of the load-of-shite variety, only fit for a barrel of keech; to have been dropped into such. She said, Oh well, you can always get another one. You're always saying it's a rotten job. So, ye can get another one.

Oh yeh …

You always say you can.

Sure. Jobs dont grow on bushes, but I can always get one.

She drew the cardigan across her shoulders. Can I talk to you or not?

I wasnt being sarcastic.

Cath nodded.

I wasnt.

Sorry, she said. Now she smiled but it occurred to me that the way to describe this smile was 'sad', she 'smiled sadly'.

No, I said, I'm sorry.

I dont know what to say.

There is nothing to say. I raised my eyebrows and scratched my head in a gesture that used to make her smile, reminding her not so much of Laurel and Hardy but the skinny half of the duo, for I, dear reader, am a wee skinny bastard.

What? said Cath.

I shall just have to apologize to the shit, the gaffer.

She smiled.

Honestly. I said, That is what I'll do, I'll walk in tonight and I shall go up and see him immediately. Excuse me, I shall say, and he shall look at me and …

It was difficult to utter the next bit because no next bit existed. Cath was waiting.

I should apologize, I said, really, because it was me that was out of order. I attacked him in front of other people. Like a humiliation nearly. He would have regarded it as such.

Oh.

I sat on the edge of the bed, reached for her hand, stared into the palm holding the edge of the tips of her beautiful fingers. I shall tell you your fortune, oh mistress of mine, oh mistress of the flowers, you shall go on a long voyage, you shall be accompanied by a small balding stranger who is

You are not balding.

Yes I am, face it, I refer here to your husband, to wit, myself.

She laughed lightly but was worried. She squeezed my hand. You dont tell fortunes in the right hand, that's the one you are born with.

Honestly?

Yeh.

I stared into her right palm, now her left, compared the two. Well well well, I said, and I aye thought they were the same. So, perchance, this explains the ill winds that blow always in my direction.

Cath smiled.

The truth is … I half smiled.

What? she said.

I dont think I can handle working these days my dear. It is all just cowards and bullies. One is surrrounded by them. Ye cannay even talk in case it gets reported.

They wont all be like that.

Nearly. Times have changed. I cannot talk to these blokes, I cannay actually talk to them. Except about football maybe, I can join in then, fucking football. I closed my eyes, speaking rapidly: Sometimes I want to do him damage. I'm talking physical stuff like battering him across the skull, that is what I'm talking about, dirty evil bastard – telling ye Cath I'm working away and my head's full of scenarios, I'll be down the stores and way at the back and he comes along, he doesnt know I'm there, I hide behind the stacks of platforms, then when he appears I jump out and smack, across the back of the skull, a shifting spanner or something, a big file maybe, I hit him with it, crunch.

That is horrible.

I smiled.

It's the way animals behave.

I nodded.

You wouldnt stoop to that?

Not at all, I said, and couldnay hide the grin which must have lit up my entire fizzog as they say in US detective stories. But that is how it gets ye and ye wind up as cowardly as the rest of them, little shit that he is – I mean metaphorically – he is not little at all. Nowadays ye do not get little gaffers. Physical intimidation is part of the job. Honest. I dont even think he is a coward. They say bullies are cowards at heart. I'm unconvinced by that. I think we just like to think it is the case, it cheers us up. I hate even looking at the guy, if he is talking to me, I cannot bear it, honestly, I cannay; I just cannay fucking bear it. It is like I might vomit over him as we converse.

Physical intimidation! I wish he would try that, I said, fucking ratbag, then we would find out. Seriously though, I am going to take him on. This time he is not getting away with it.

I stopped, the way Cath was looking at me.

I know what ye're thinking, I said.

Then I'll not say it.

I nodded, studying the lines in the palm of her hand.
Abracabranksi!

I said that to make her smile. I used it with my lasses
when they were wee. That is the one magic word above
all. Abracabranski. The lasses thought I was kidding.
But I wasnt, like the best magic it was secret; nobody
else knew it, just us, us.

Cath was unsmiling. Yes, she said, I shall say it,
because I have to. Why does it have to be you? Why
does it have to be you? Are you the only one? Why is it
you? Why does it have to be you?

Why does what have to be me?

You know what.

I dont.

She stared at me.

I dont. I dont. Eh …

Why are ye smiling?

Smiling?

But I had smiled. What she said was true. Even as we
spoke I was smiling. Two reasons:

1] She thought nice things about me concerning
the opposite of moral cowardice
2] She performed a movement of her shoulders
that was characteristic.

Naybody else in the whole world did it. Except her
grannie. But she had died ten years back. Cath was
alone. Unless the lasses maintained the tradition. Still
and all I found it weird how this one solitary manoeuvre
might force me into saying things I did not want to say.

I refer to commitments. I did not want to commit myself to a single damn thing!

What is it? she said.

What is what?

You shook your head.

Oh did I?

She sighed.

Cath, it doesnay matter.

What doesnt?

I unclasped my wristwatch, laid it on the mantelpiece. I reached to switch on the radio but paused, and asked first. Mind if I put on the radio?

I would prefer if ye didnt.

Aw.

If ye dont mind.

Of course

I'm going to lie down, she said.

She had taken the cardigan from her shoulders, she laid it along the foot of the bed. She did this to keep her feet warm. I lifted the cardigan and returned it to her bedside chair, and replaced it with a smallish blanket.

Thanks, she said without smiling, and added, Did ye go to the pub?

I told you I didnt.

You were a bit late home.

Yeh.

She continued watching me.

I shrugged. She was waiting. I just walked up and down, I said. I got off the bus and just eh, I walked up and down for a wee bit; coming to terms with things I suppose.

So you did get sacked.

I returned her look then glanced at the radio. No fancy a bit of music?

But she was not going to give up, gony gie up, she wasnay gony. People are strange. Wives especially; their tenacity makes them doubly so. I wonder if they are like that with other women, or is it just with men. It aint a question. I call it a noggin-shaker, as in 'one shakes one's noggin'.

Cath, I said, I need to say something: it was important what happened with that shit. I'm no taking crap off the likes of him. What because he's my gaffer I'm supposed to shut my mouth! Never. It is not life or death, granted, but we still cannay allow it. I am not going to allow it. Right-wing fucking bastard, I am telling ye, guys like him, Labour Party bastards, they put the Tories to shame, fascist cunts. That is who they put in charge, that is so-called Britain and the fucking ppolitical system.

Cath watched from the safety of the sheets and duvet.

But it is a serious thing, I said, we are talking here about working-class representation. Bloody joke.

Yes well write yer book, she said, ye've wasted enough time.

I shall write it.

Fine.

Some of us are not going stand for it any longer. I mean are we supposed to let them walk ower the top of us? Fucking bunch of gangsters. You think I'm past it, well I'm no past it. If you think I am, I'm no.

No what, past what, did I miss something?

I dont actually care, I said, honestly, I dont. I'm forty-two years of age. Do ye know what we talk about during a typical tea-break in one's typical factory warehouse? How effing glad we shall be to reach one's seniority; in other words our chief desire is to become old-age pensioners. What happened to all our hopes and dreams! That is what happened to them. This is what I am talking about, give me the happy pills. Great Britain today, the existential nightmare that would have driven my poor old father off his fucking nut if he hadnay had the good sense to die at the advanced age of sixty-one and three quarters. So-called Scotland, be it known, a complete waste of space: I refer here to one's existence.

I wish I was a pensioner already. I want to go to a green field and just lie down. I want to get put out to graze like these old horses that win the Grand National, nay hustle and bustle, just chewing the cud. Mind you, I said, pausing with one's hand on the bedroom door handle. I would like to get him. Preferably down the back of the storeroom, thoughts of shifting spanners and skulls, crunch de la crunch.

Cath was looking worried re sanity, her partner's.

You dont know whether to believe me or not, I said.

He certainly is getting to you.

Oh jees.

He is.

Yeh, I said, I wake up thinking about him, go to sleep thinking about him. Fucking ratbag! Ach well. Want a cup of tea?

Eh …

Hot water with lemon?

How did ye guess?

I smiled. I'm gony have toast, d'ye no want some? Take some toast. The little essentials in life, toast and marmalada madame, eh, you want, you want me I serve you brekadafast ladeee, my leetil dandeelion senorita.

Cath looked at me.

Ye sure? I said.

No thanks.

Sorry about this stupid male shite.

Mm.

I continued into the kitchen, filled the kettle, standing next to the sink. And the window. From here I looked straight upwards, over the tenement roofs facing. It was a flight path. I enjoyed seeing the planes, these long-haul destinations, desert islands and nice hotels. Month holidays. People needed month holidays in foreign domains. No bosses, no gaffers, no Scottishness or Britishness.

There was a sound behind. Her arms were round me while I was dumping the teabag into one's mug. I stopped what I was doing. She held me tightly. She was wearing only her nightdress. I cannot move, I said.

I'm not letting ye move.

You are so warm and cuddly.

Just relax.

I have to get the milk, I said.

Relax.

I did relax. After a moment I sighed. My shoulders drooped. Man, fuck, I felt it, man, for fuck sake man oh man gaffers and all sorts, out the fucking windi amazing, how I felt, how it happened. I heard the water approach boiling point and freed my right arm, ready to pour it into the mugs. That is our rightful tradition, I said, to be felt by others as we feel them

You just cannot relax, she said.

I can, I'm just eh preparing to pour the water.

She sighed, irritated. She was, and it was my fault. She walked to collect her cigarettes. They were next to the microwave. We had a wee hi-fi system beside it. Not fancy some music? Put something on, I said.

What?

Anything.

What like?

I scratched down beneath the lobe of my ear then my scalp, watching her light a cigarette. She had a range of nightdresses. They were all kind of silly, with bunny-rabbit patterns, teddy bears. With her figure they were a bit incongruous, thank christ, she didnay have what they call a girlish figure. She skipped through the CDs, barely reading their covers. The Karelia's a cassette, I said.

Oh I'm not playing a cassette.

Well whatever, whatever ye like.

You always want Sibelius.

I dont always want Sibelius, I'll take Hazel Dickens.

If you want the cassette go and get it. I can never find anything in there, it's a complete mess.

I watched her inhale on the cigarette, a really long sort of deep inhalation as befits one who enjoys a smoke, like myself, who wrapped it all in a year ago and have regretted it ever since, unlike one's nearest and dearest who has a fancy card pinned on the wall which reads: This belongs to a Happy Smoker!

Hurrch! That is what I shout whenever I see it. Now she gied me a wifely look. Is that smoke good? I said.

She winked.

Blow it ower here will ye! I clutched at the smoke and inhaled loudly. Ye know something, I said, things havenay been the same in the factory since Jimmy Robertson retired.

Mm.

That's the truth.

Cath nodded.

I mean really, old Jimmy, christ. You never saw him but ye knew he was there. That last year, they put him out in the gatehouse.

That wasnt fair.

I nodded.

It wasnt.

Naw. Although he preferred it … he said he did anyway – fuck, that guy was a beacon. Ye aye knew: here is one guy that still exists in the world, a proper reader, a proper thinker, somebody that knows pppolitics and fucking fuck knows what, history! Everything!

Dont look for excuses.

Excuses for what?

To finish with yer job. If ye want to finish the job then finish it.

I am finished with it.

Cath smiled at me for a moment.

I am finished with it, I said.

Oh.

I didnt think you were listening to me.

I was.

I am finished with it.

She nodded.

At least with Jimmy I could talk about stuff. See that crowd nowadays, they are so ignorant. But they think they know everything. They actually believe the Scottish Nationalists are a left-wing party, them and the Lib Dems. Honest! At the same time but if ye want to vote socialist ye vote for the Labour Party. Unless ye're an extremist. In that case ye vote for the Scottish Socialists! Honest, that's what they think. Ye ever heard such crap! But they actually believe it.

Cath sighed.

They know nothing so they cannay think. They cannay think because they know nothing.

She might have been listening to me. She lifted an ashtray from the mantelpiece, planked herself down on the one armchair in the entire room, laying the ashtray beside her on the shoogly fucking wee coffee table that aye collapsed if I even looked at the stupid thing. She pulled her legs up, covering her shoulders with a woolly article, tugging the nightdress down to cover her legs. She inhaled on the cigarette and shivered. I was about to walk to her but my foot kicked a teddy bear. Imagine that, a teddy bear. My daughters were ten and twelve and they still fucked about with teddy bears.

I hated using the word 'fuck' when referring to one's offspring. But there we are.

Look at that, I said, and stooped to pick it up. It's got one of these ears ye see on the *Antiques Roadshow*.

No it doesnt.

It's probably worth an effing fortune!

If it's got a button in the ear. Only if.

Is that right?

Yeh.

Christ.

Cath smiled.

Why dont you go to nightschool and do a course on antiques? I think you could earn a fortune. You have a feel for it. At the same time …

Yes?

I shrugged.

Cath was looking at me.

Fancy a go?

What?

Nothing.

You're so edgy.

I'm not.

Then ye jump down my throat.

I dont really, it's just the way it comes out. Things get to me. I try not to let them but they do. Just now they do. It's no to do with being edgy, I just get a tight feeling.

Oh so you want me to worry about heart attacks?

Not at all. I raised my hand to my upper chest and rubbed in a circular motion.

She watched me. Have ye got indigestion?

A touch.

She swung her legs down from the seat. She said, I take it ye were talking about sex?

Who me?

I know you.

You know me!

I do.

Ye think ye know me.

Okay, she said, but were you talking about sex?

Yes but we'll have a drink of tea first.

She swung her legs back on to the seat. Called yer bluff as usual.

I chuckled, passing her a mug of hot water with a dod of lemon floating about.

Just relax, she said, for a change.

My feet will be freezing.

Good.

What d'ye mean good!

Cath smiled. Wash them, that will heat them up. They're probably ponging.

Oh man.

Some people would go for a shower.

But I'm just finished my work!

Dont wheedle.

Well really, I'm not wheedling. I paused, smiled in a conspiratorial manner. You think you've got the upper hand dont you?

She exhaled smoke towards me. I awaited her comment. None came. I closed my eyes. I thought she might have spoken then but she didnt. Thus I would have to.

No. I didnt have to, not at all. Of course I didnt, nobody is obliged to speak. Sometimes I cannay get the hang of that obvious truth, people like me, we cant. And evil fuckers like the gaffer play on it. I honest. Will we ever be free of the shite, the degradation – because that is what it is, degradation. We are degraded man! Will they ever leave us alone? Ye wonder but.

Cath gazed at me.

Ye know what he called me? a throwback; he called me a throwback.

What did you do?

Me?

Yes.

What did I do? I cannot remember.

Is he afraid of you?

You joking?

I wouldnt be too sure.

He's paranoiac right enough.

There ye are, said Cath.

He thinks I've got the young team on my side.

Who?

The younger ones. He thinks they listen to me. They do but only about football; only if I dont lecture them about ppppolitics; they cannay cope with ppppolitics.

Cath listened but was not smiling. I saw the anxiety. Smoke didnt relax her. I was glad I had stopped.

I wished I could help her stop. I wished I could help her period. Just about the future, I wasnay sure about the future. It was a long time till I retired. Maybe we could go someplace. Anyway, she was going back to work herself. If she could get a job. She spoke about getting a job but how did she know she would get one, she didnay even know she would get one, fucking dreamworld.

Oh man.

What is it? she said.

I spoke out loud eh …! I smiled. Come here, take a look outside the window. Come on! Take a look! Blue sky … nothing but blue sky.

She made no move. She held the mug of tea in her right hand, close by her cheek. I like the way women do that; every last ounce of heat, ye want to extract it.

Intract it, she said.

Intract it! Take it out and put it in.

Dont be vulgar.

I smiled. Cath puffed on her cigarette. Or interact, I said. That must be where the word comes from.

Where's the toast? Did ye not make toast? I thought ye were hungry?

To be honest, no.

I'll make ye something.

Dont bother.

I'll just finish my smoke first.

I can make it myself.

Cath smiled. I watched her inhale again on the cigarette. Two puffs in two seconds. What if she died? I nodded. If you dont stop smoking you will die. Do ye know that?

She blew smoke at me. I grinned and shouted at the ceiling. Heh God! There's a woman down here trying to kill herself!

Cath covered her mouth with her right hand: Oh ya blaspheming pig ye, you'll go to hell.

She was really laughing and I laughed too. I swallowed some tea, set the mug on the arm of the chair, then transferred it to the floor. She was watching me. I reached down and lifted it, transferred it to a safer place, the damn table.

Good boy.

I saluted her. Mon capitaine. I returned to the window. There are scarecrows down below skipper. Think I should toss them a lifeline? I cupped my hand to my mouth: Leave them to suffer bosun, leave them to suffer! It's the only way they'll learn. Aye aye sir!

What ye blethering about!

Nothing, I'm just cracking up.

Linda's coming home at dinner time.

What about dinner-school?

She asked to stay off.

My god. In my day we would have gave wur eyeteeth for school dinners.

Cath was stubbing her cigarette out.

Far below the window the docile subjects wended their weary way back and forward and back and forward.

Is that you talking to yerself again!

I always think of that painting by Breughel, the one with all the people, and the horses and dogs; the village scene.

You're wrong to think of that one.

How come?

Because it is the slaughter of the innocents.

Christ, aye.

Your memory is not good.

I know, it is like a mental collapse has occurred. My synapses have collapsed. Death by collapsing synapses. For all I know it's a recognized industrial disease, brought on by constant nightshift.

We need to get away.

Mayo!

Not Ireland.

I'd love to go to Ireland.

Not me.

I wish we could.

We cant.

What about the Hebrides?

Oh god.

Sorry.

I just wish …

What?

Nothing.

I closed my eyes tightly. There are choices to make and we've got to make the right yin. We do, we have to! I slapped my forehead with my right hand, then again. And this time a real fucking sore yin and it made a loud slapping noise. Jesus christ, I said, that was sair!

Dont expire yet.

I gave an exaggerated groan, clutching at my chest: They're taking my life's blood, the last breath in me body.

Relax. Come to bed.

I'll no sleep.

Ye will.

I'll have to masturbate and I'm too old to masturbate. Honest, I blush when I do it

Ye're just exhausted, yer last shift of the week.

My last shift period.

Oh so ye have been sacked!

I smiled. I opened the window wider, to let out the tobacco fug. Not to jump, I said, to let in some air. I feel kind of jittery, like I'm defenceless.

I scratched my mouth, wiped round it quite roughly. It is true, I am defenceless. The next time the gaffer looks at me the wrong way I'm liable to burst out greeting. That is the kind of man I am, the kind of guy you're married to.

I like the guy I'm married to.

Naw but nay kidding ye Cath … I stopped and stared out the window, straining to see farther below, my head angling. My goodness look at that, I said.

What, what are you looking at?

God knows.

Is she attractive?

Not as attractive as you. I faced her now, folding my arms. You thought I was past it?

Past what?

Would ye leave me if I was?

You do get some juvenile ideas.

I shook my head, looked back out the window. Sometimes I just want to lie and stare up at the sky, see if I can spot some stars.

During the day?

Sure, why not? If ye want to look and see ye should be able to ... I wiped spittle from the corner of my mouth. I could do with a smoke myself.

Well you're not getting one, she said.

I dont want one.

That's all we need, you starting again.

It's the smell ...

Cath smiled. She left her cigarette smouldering in the ashtray and came towards me. I made space for her to see out the window, put my arm round her shoulder. Far below a woman was passing along the pavement and entering our very close. It made us both smile. I find that very positive, I said.

Cath chuckled.

Who is she? I said.

Missis Taylor, she lives one up.

Honestly?

Yeh.

God! I laughed.

She looked at me steadily, unsmiling. I kissed her on the forehead, cupped her chin in my hand, angling my head to kiss her on the lips. She was always so cool, so calm, but I could never have told her that, never.

And she wouldnt have believed me, she didnt believe me, it wasnt true, it was just shite, it was nonsense. I broke from her and she frowned, then smiled. What's up?

Nothing, I said.

On Becoming a Reader

by rail daily to school, thus my penchant for departing
class prior to the schoolday's rightful conclusion that I
might not disintegrate through the unutterable
boredom of the subjects under consideration, my
being forced to consider these subjects that I might the
better advance beyond my fellows on the hierarchical
ladder that was the greatbritishsocialsystem, the place
of my parents and family not deemed of the lower
orders but affixed therein through no fault of our own
how-somever the school subjects under consideration
purported to bring about the opportunity of escape,
nor yet the fault of my parents whose apparent
acceptance of this greatbritishsocialsystem ceded to
myself a marked nauseousness largely indescribable
but by authors whose ability to transcend that same
indescribability by virtue of the act of storytelling
exhibited not only the sad limits of an inferior art but
an open-armed adherence to that system, inducing
within myself a consolidation of purpose, effected by
that same nauseousness, the predictable outcome of
right reasoning, my unconscionable assumption of the
dubiety of all adult authority, my consequent
contempt being ill-concealed, barely disguised, leaving
withdrawal from that society my only duty, the last

straw being the charred remains of a book I had
purchased, found in the fireplace, having been
adjudged licentious by my mother and set in flames,
though the book were purchased on my own account
by means of a monetary gift from a grandmother, that
was mine and mine alone to do as wish should take
me, so that now, approaching a birthdate of more
than passing interest its being the age by which a
youth may decree that the departure of the education
system is the one route by which the guarantee of
sanity may be

as if from nowhere

I reached for the notepad from the back end of the cabinet. Nurse Liddell and colleague had entered the ward. The cabinet was by the side of the bed. I only had to reach, it was very convenient. Of course it was convenient for god sake I was hospitalized, a patient. Awaiting the results of further tests! Oh the drama, the drama!

Yes. One eschewed negativity. To hell with negativity. This is what one uttered, within the sanctity of one's own brain.

Still and all, still and all. The truth. Yes the truth; breathe in and breathe out: the truth is I knew it was not good, I was not good. Otherwise, otherwise I would not have been there, not like this.

Something less than good.

Good!

What other terms do we have? Pleasant. Nice. Joyous. Smashing. What else? I could not think of many more. Unlike bad. Evil, crappy, unpleasant, shit, horrible, terrible, malevolent, worsening, maleficent, malodorous, pestilent, horrendous. Hell's bells, a million of them. Thus the human condition. But truly, my condition was not great, otherwise

oh man, man man, man man man

I opened my eyes. I had to. It is good to open the eyes; one's eyes; mine; my fucking eyes.

I reached again for the notepad, to hell with it man, one reaches for it, grasps. Impaired memory. The lapse into melancholia was to be guarded against and one did. One guarded against it. One exercised oneself, one's faculties. Yet reaching for the notepad happened prior to the thought itself. A surely remarkable phenomenon. Ergo

Now aware of the intestines. Interrupting the thought, the last thought. Aware of my intestines.

In what respect aware: simply aware, that is all. But overwhelmingly so.

What about them? Clogged tubes. Clogged tubes.

The chart hung on the rail at the foot of the bed. If only I could read it. Telescopes: patients are not supplied with them thus one cannot read from a distance. But for something horrendous why not inform the patient? Patients too are people.

I used a notebook to monitor the situation, noting symptoms, physical changes, thoughts, feelings. Anything at all. Wee doodles and drawings. Any damn thing I pleased. It was my damn notepad and my damn situation; my physicality. Drawings. Any damn thing.

I wanted to draw a face. Why not. Yes. In summation of my plight I would draw a face.

I knew a face. A face. I knew a face. Where was the pencil? My thought of the moment as pictorial representation: set it down set it down set it down. Urgency urgency fucking pencil the nurse had removed the damn thing as per fucking usual stop swearing.

Who is swearing. Okay. Behind the cup. The pencil lay behind the cup. The nurse may have nudged it. I myself, I myself. I reached towards it, towards the pencil.

The tension! My heavens. Absolute – as between the pencil and the urine sample, not to knock them over, the shaky hand, the quivering knuckles.

Knuckles? My fucking knuckles! The knuckles of late middle age. Prehistoric-looking things; tiny clumps of black hair. How in the name of that which aspires to holiness do children consent to hold such a hand!

Even more astonishing, that a woman should allow such a hand to touch her skin, stroke her skin, to trace, these lines and surface of the skin who ever drew the surface of the skin, had any artist ever managed that. The greatest artists are the greatest but who among them had ever succeeded in drawing the surface of the skin oh my merciful heavens, the density of this, this skin. Skin is a surface.

It is. If the thought ever occurred in the past it had gone from my memory, vanished into that internal and all-encompassing ether which maketh manifest one's internal space. But what does 'manifest' mean!

The urine sample. Even here in the hospital bed we surmount obstacles. Was it not crazy? All of it was. See the hand, the pencil, the bottle. Yea though I did reach it without mishap.

If I had gone to the lavatory I would have experienced pain. What about the pain, or pains. Pains growing from my belly or were they in from my belly, its lining. If the cancer was there, cancer of the lining of the belly.

What else could it be! Tell him tell him tell him! he screamed.

I refer to myself. Do not keep the patient in the dark. We have to deal with eternity so give us a break with that which may be known, that can be rendered manifest.

Manifest? There we have it again.

A boulder come to rest. I imagined it wedged there, the cancer entity, unyielding. I would have had to swallow it. How had I managed this! The journey down my gullet. But it had sunk and was at rest until then began its movement. The movement of the cancer entity. Feel my cancer. Touch it. This living thing, a growth that is organic but not organic. But it must feed. Upon what must it feed? Why, one's entrails, one's intestines, one's blood and tissue, one's bonemarrow; all manner of edible substances. One's body is a feast, veritably so. Tumours grow and spread. How come? How come I had never learned about the subject? Not properly. Surely it should have been required reading for all. People die of cancer every second. If cancer it was. Of course it was.

So why had I not gone before? Had fate been smiling upon me!

Was I one of the lucky ones. Oy yez oy yez. Read all about it.

What are the statistics? Horrible.

Why had my parents not emigrated from this godforsaken hellhole where death and disease and malformity

Or grandparents! What kind of grandparents were they! Did they even deserve such a nomenclature! Ancient old bastards. No, they were undeserving. They were not grandparents at all. Not-so-grand-parents, this is what they were. Cowards. Why did everybody not emigrate. At an early age. Maybe they preferred to die young. Cowards cowards and again cowards. Them and their fucking offspring. Die die!

The damn notepad. Draw a face. Whose face?

Or the urine sample, I reached for that instead of the notepad and would have held it to my lips. Yes. Might one die from drinking urine? Of course not. Especially not one's own. You would just seem like a pervert. But not if it was your own. Then you would just be mad. Mad! I'm mad I tell you, mad!

Look, the guy's mad. He has a ghastly expression on his countenance.

Drinking piss. What a life. Cancer is better than that. At least I had my brains, they had not been gnawed. I imagined the movement of the cancer to resemble a gnawing activity.

There are these myriad afflictions we humans experience. All sorts of them. I was fortunate never to have had more than a couple. Not the worst. Not even close to the worst. A quaffer of urine! Oh mercy mercy, mercy me.

But apparently mothers did this of their offspring. They expressed an urge to quaff their babies' piss and some went ahead and did it. They kissed their babies' bums! Or was it licked? My god surely not! They held their babies up and rubbed their noses in their wee bums! Incredible behaviour. Yet womanly, motherly. Apparently.

A wee baby's bum. What is wrong with that, they have had their bath and there they are all nice and clean and laughing away or gurgling. Babies gurgle.

You would hardly describe such behaviour as perverted; not if it pertained to mummy, performed in the maternal spirit. But take some unshaven unkempt middle-aged grandpappy cunt. In other words I myself. I would get fucking lynched man!

Fate.

Or else had one been a murderer, slave to the baser forms of violence; a wild beast, acutely dangerous to other human beings, and that violence was directed against children and very elderly invalids. One of these dirty evil bastards whose testicles one would willingly chop to safeguard others. Damn right. I would wield the axe. I had no compunction. I would shovel the ashes into the chamber, out of the chamber, whatever it took. Slam shut the door sir slam shut the door. It tolleth for you, you.

Along the way I saw Nurse Liddell; she was talking to her colleague, she was telling a tale. That humour in her voice. And most beautiful pair of legs. Nurse Liddell from Ghana, gesturing with her hands and moving on her feet. That old cliché, full of life. Her colleague was also from Africa but another country. That was a guess. Maybe it was the same one. She was listening, nodding, grinning; more pal than colleague.

I knew of Nurse Liddell that she was in love with her family and could not contemplate life without them. Her telling of the tales of her life established the fact. Her wider family; cousins and uncles and aunts, nieces and nephews: all interested her, each with a story to tell. Little did she know they told stories of her. She made them all laugh. She made them chuckle with pleasure. Also she was so damnably attractive. One experienced the urge to fling one's arms about her, around her, her shoulders and just her person, really. There are such women. One marches towards them and there go the arms: I am not responsible! Forgive me forgive me!

But one's arms are already there, the action performed.

I crave your pardon milady. My physical parts are autonomous. Causation my dear. The action an effect of your presence. You caused the action. You are the mover. Bang. And the action is created.

Whenever Nurse Liddell entered the ward there was movement below and it wasnt no tumour, god damn, no sir. Whenever that movement occurred I knew she was in the vicinity: the penis had raised his head.

Ugly. Ugly ugly. But that too! The pencil, behind the cup. I gulped saliva aware of a tenderness at the back of my throat.

My notepad from the cupboard, I lifted it across. What effort!

Why the exhaustion!

Why the pencil what the thought. Rawness and effort, tenderness at the back of the throat. Ugly ugly.

I entered symptoms and feelings, hunger, lust. Lust theoretical. But theoretical or no, lust was crucial lust was life lust was

breathe in breathe out

good

Call the nurse. Excuse me, I believe you are monitoring my condition. I have to advise you, I am experiencing great lust, albeit theoretical.

Insolent bastard. Slap.

How to begin. I had no energy for this. Thoughts and pencils. The penis raised its head. Ugly ugly. I would draw it instead. The drawn penis is not so bad.

I used the pencil. It was not a lung disease. Why had I thought that. Because it was true.

The Nurse with the Beautiful Legs. Beautiful Boobs too. 'Boobs' is not my word: 'tits' is my word. My wife was coming to visit and if she spotted 'tits' she would wonder. She was not a woman for 'tits', that sort of word, it spoiled things, life, the life one shares. She would see the notepad, the drawn penis.

Goodness me. Oh well, 'twas her right.

I could have smiled. But a dust mite caught in my throat, I coughed into the top sheet. A dry cough, a rawness. Rawness. I wrote down the word, and noted it from a previous page. The female shape, her head and shoulders again, down her body, sketching fast, her legs. It was the nurse, I was drawing the nurse. She could take the breath away. Othertimes no, no. On the street one could pass her by, pass her by.

I dont believe it, I really dont believe it. Yes. Yes.

But she wore the uniform just right. Appositely. And nothing under it bar skimpy stockings and all of that and when she leaned over to make the bed oh my dear her legs, they went right up her body, as far as her, well now, well now indeed.

What shit. Pathetic.

But true, true. And women also appreciated Nurse Liddell because what an appetite for life this lassie had. This lassie had it definitely. Even her shoes! I liked her shoes. They were maybe uniform shoes but somehow, what the hell had she done? it was like she had acquired the design of the basic uniform shoe and embellished it in some way connected to the design itself, the very lines of a shoe, of any shoe, the leather surface. Leather is skin and skin is surface.

Babble babble. I babbled, babble babble.

Yakking to her colleague and pal; that old saying, nineteen to the dozen. And her colleague and pal delighting in Nurse Liddell's yarn, acutely aware of how lucky she was, oh how lucky, to be here in Europe instead of back home amid the dust and food short-ages, disease and corruption, the political jiggery-pokery. It would have killed me.

Had I been African I would not have sought asylum, I would not have left my country. I would have remained and fought until the last gasp expired from my body.

Why did people not fight? It was the same in Scotland. People didnt fight, not like in the old days. Scots wha hae. Nowadays it was just like whatever it was, acceptance, submission, grovellation, to a bunch of corrupt administrators, lawyers and bureaucrats whose debased self-interest enabled the undead not to colonize the world, but to enslave it. Well not me. Oh no, I would fight. I certainly would fight. I did fight. I still did fight and would fight and continue to do so, indeed I would, though the pain wracked, dried and drained my very soul, aarghh, the last gasp from my spent frame.

There are many ways to fight. Yes there are weapons but also there are penises. Penises! I mean pens, pens. And applied in the correct way there is nothing more powerful than a dame than a pen. Take your sword and shove it, give me a pen.

But the rape and attempted murder of an entire continent, a continent so huge that an airflight across one country takes five hours. Way up north, deserts and nothing: nomad hunters and shimmering shifting sands. I heard an African writer declare on radio that Europe would not be satisfied until the extermination of the last African. Europe demanded Africa. And when I said Europe was I including America? Why certainly. And Australia, and Israel. And the part of Africa that was Europe, what about it? Why, my dear fellow, concealed from the argument. Europe demanded Africa. Its minerals and markets, its coast and sandy beaches, strategic primacy, safari parks, the sun going down and the servant brings one a cocktail, one reclines on a hammock, meek docility, she wears a sarong tied loosely, her hair piled high on her head, she may smile, mysteriously – at her husband who is out of view, hiding to the side of the thatched hut, eyes dead in your direction, well you may tense.

But the word 'boobs' is ludicrous. 'Boobs'.

One charts the mind of a human being, one discovers the absurdity therein. The absurdity of existence as contained within one human frame. Of one human being; examine one and you find absurdity.

Nurse Liddell and colleague moved toward the patient directly across from me. I knew the fellow's name but could not remember it – old Mister Somebody. He was on his last legs. Middle-aged persons came a-visiting and the young, the grandchildren. They stood beside the bed, trying not to touch the covers lest they too contracted the disease. Joe Smith had visited him regularly. Joe.

Where was Joe? What had happened to Joe? Where the hell was he who forswore his own illness for the good of the hospital?

Actually Joe was a good man and there is no point me being facetious about this. He walked about 'cheering' everybody up. Such people exist. Joe was one of them. Some people who do that are horrible evangelical patronizing fucking egotistical bastards. Not Joe. Joe is or was genuine. Probably he had dropped dead.

Hell's bells.

The notepad and pencil rested between my left leg and the edge of the bed.

I had lain them to rest. Were one to shift position they might tumble to the floor.

Fraught!

I refer to one's life. Even here, within the confines of the hospital bed, one experienced the existential nightmare of that which we know as the day-to-day.

Nurse Liddell speaking to her colleague, and quietly, the patient might have heard had he not been snoozing, old Mister Somebody, bereft of consciousness. He could not hear, alas. Nineteen twentieths of the old fellow's life passed in sleep. His body was drained, his lifeforce spent, in defence against the cancer entity. I saw it as a war; a small and well-drilled army takes on a huge, densely populated country. Sooner or later one or more limbs of the well-drilled army will fail. They cannot continue indefinitely

unequal struggle

Compos mentis, however. I remained so, alert. Why then had I sighed? I had sighed. Why had I sighed and so damnably tired so damnably damnably tired so tired so tired

The notepad and pencil, and close to the edge. When had I laid them to rest?

No major event. Nothing was. The nurses were young women. The men they liked were so much younger than me, much younger, very much younger. One saw them on television. Confident young males, they all were confident and boyish. Boyish! They were all so fucking boyish, it made one grue, at their so-called charms, stylish in their disarray. But still the girls smiled upon them. No doubt

No doubt. I had tacked on the 'no doubt' as a form of reassurance. The typically pathetic manoeuvre of the older male, pretending a righteous displeasure at the antics of the young, when it was nothing more than the deepest most god-awful jealousy, and bitterness. I could have killed, and I would have, these fuckers.

Whence the anger?

I was not beyond the pale. The nurses were in their mid-twenties, so that made how many years of a difference? countless and countless were a lot, a lot of years, as they say, a vast pressure of water rushing beneath the bridge.

And propped up on all these pillows; this is what the vast pressure of water had done to me. Swimming against the tide, or with the tide, it made no difference. The exhaustion was one. An unimaginable

the thought itself unimaginable. And as I began reaching for the notepad even my god my arms, even them, as though aching. Arms ached, but I pushed forwards one, my right, oh god, groaning aloud, and in the next bed the man moved his feet.

This man had been asleep and seemed always to be so but now was awake.

Because I had groaned! Yes!

I held my breath, looking to the mound wherein lay my belly beneath the sheets. Better the devil one knows than the unknown evil thing lurking in the dark, enabled to perform its malevolence. I looked for the nurses, their voices no longer audible.

They had gone.

My pillows were stuffed together! They propped me up! They had been plumped! My pillows. Someone had done the plumping chore. While I was not looking. Was that possible!

So there we are. One is reduced

What time now?

But who had plumped up the damn pillows? God damn.

The smell of food.

I was to receive food and the sense of it was to the fore. What might it be? No matter, I would savour it. I always did. My wife derided me for that. My sons didnt. It was a gender issue. And I hailed from a large family. Members of large families savour food. They fight for food. They die, die for food

however

No however, howevers. The food would come to me and the auxiliary staff person would not see me while serving.

A tired woman. I could draw her, her face. She concentrated on the work. I would have communicated with this woman. I would encourage her smile. I would remark in an amusing manner as to the nature of the world, a Stoical perspective assumed, and she would respond to that.

Nor need communication imply a new relationship. Tomorrow she could resume her normal working practices in silence, her blinkers donned, oblivious to one's maleness; not any maleness, simply that of the patient, one's humanity.

I would so advise her. Do not nullify our existence. Nor is there a need to worry; and certainly not about me. Who has the energy for such nonsense? let alone hospitalized parties the likes of myself. Even prior to the present situation, and location, I was not the man to overstep the mark, certainly not.

I would prefer being elsewhere. No harm in such a confession.

The list of dietary details. Nought special for me. I ate anything, red butchermeat a delight. Even salad. Ho hum. I studied the leaves and other food. Oh well. But when I lifted my fork I found that I could not eat. I pushed a forkful of cold meat and lettuce to my mouth, into my mouth, but could not nibble.

There was no space in my stomach. Where could I put the food? If I swallowed what would happen? Would the meat and lettuce settle in my throat. Perhaps if I masticated thoroughly the food might squeeze its way down. But my goodness it surely was a nonsense. Was I expected to cope. How could I.

A fellow patient could no longer swallow. The food settled between his cheeks and gums and was a concern for the medical staff should a particle have entered the lungs, pneumonia? something like that. I watched for signs myself. But I was nowhere near that stage.

My stomach should have had space aplenty for food. In recent days I had eaten less than normal. So why should it now be full? I reached for the notepad. Any phenomena, any at all.

Nurse Liddell materialized. I prepared to smile but she did not glance in my direction. She returned to the bed nearest the window, old Mister Somebody – McGuire.

The nurses called me him, but they called Mister McGuire old Mister McGuire.

Old Mister McGuire. How could one but pity the man. He was always asleep. Or unconscious. The staff spoke about old Mister McGuire within earshot of other patients.

Beyond earshot what did they call me? Him. But apart from him. The good-looking older guy!

Has the good-looking older guy been given his bedbath this morning?

Bedbath. A fantasy for many. Joe Smith always referred to bedbaths in his wee chats. But he was wrong: such events take place free of erections. The nurses, in full professionalism, merely brush the insistent manifestation to one side, get thee beside thee, and dight one's thighs in a formal manner.

Poor Joe. Unless he had gone home. People did go home, and as full human beings, resuming their personhood. Each time a bed became empty I presumed the death of the patient. It was nonsense!

Joe would be missed. But even he failed to engage old Mister McGuire in conversation. Nobody managed that. Not even his middle-aged daughters who appeared most days. They did. That old man was the most regularly visited party in the entire ward. He must have been a great old fellow. Otherwise why would they all come to see him?

Because he was about to drop dead. And he was rich, and they all had an eye on the loot.

Whereas me.

Who the hell came for me! My sons were in England. And people forget. They do. I pretended indifference to my wife, if the subject arose. What did it matter if one's visitors, one's visitors

Few, very few; few, fewer and fewest, in completion of the sentence, which is life itself, life itself is the sentence

And I needed to piss to piss. But I couldnt. The need was not serious. The entire piss was psychological. It was one for the doctors' rounds.

How are you today mister errrrrr?

Oh I had a psychological piss you fucking nincompoop.

Nurse Liddell would smile. I too. Unless I frowned. I had no mirror. I wanted no mirror.

The idea of seeing oneself!

The philosophers were wrong.

If I smiled it was self-consciously done. Otherwise impossible. A horse laugh could have worked.

Another nurse was there now, alongside Nurse Liddell. Who was she? Merciful heavens. I had never seen her before. A thin skull, high cheekbones, lightly the nose, lower lip; hair – and so reminiscent, reminiscent, she was, my god, I knew this woman

and tense right shoulder tense right shoulder, I could see it from here, the line of her neck, the line of her tits; her hand rested on the patient, near to my neck. 'Twas the same, the same.

But the eyes of this nurse! Her eyes could not be drawn. Her eyes were so full of the life the life. In the most remarkable of remarkable ways, so full of life, vigorous and beautiful, moving to the other side of my bed, one wanted to kiss her, just embrace, an embrace, who was this woman

and beyond there the old fellow, Mister – who was it? – somebody, Mister Somebody, dead to the world, shot full of dope, fucking dope

The sigh was allowed. I had sighed. I sighed. Okay. Settling back on the pillow now, where the pencil, and notepad, the pencil and notepad. Close to the edge oh so close. Thank god she was not attending me, it was not a time for strange nurses.

Here lieth I, sometime known as Old I, for whisper it: this indeed is I. In sore need of a breath, perhaps so, if not breathing hardly, hardly

at all, thus might one sleep, have gone in sleep so far, so far, that the pulse, the old pulse, as when the tiredness hits, and the way such tiredness also affects, has affected, effected, so strange, how it happens, occasionally also when my wife is there, sitting by me, as if from nowhere, the plumped pillows.

Bangs & a Full Moon

A fine Full Moon from the third storey through the red reflection from the city lights: this was the view. I gazed at it, lying outstretched on the bed-settee. I was thinking arrogant thoughts of that, Full Moons, and all those awful fucking writers who present nice images in the presupposition of universal fellowship under the western Stars when all of a sudden: BANG, an object hurtling out through the window facing mine across the street.

The windows on this side had been in total blackness; the building was soon to be demolished and formally uninhabited.

BANG. An object hurtled through another window. No lights came on. Nothing could be seen. Nobody was heard. Down below the street was deserted; broken glass glinted. I returned to the bed-settee and when I had rolled the smoke, found I already had one smouldering in the ashtray. I got back up again and closed the curtains. I was writing in pen & ink so not to waken the kids and wife with the banging of this machine I am now using.

A Sour Mystery

The security entrance buzzer sounded. It was somebody who used to be a friend, a firm friend; what they
call an 'intimate' friend. Obviously I invited her in. Otherwise things would have gone from bad to worse. She
was there to give me her troubles. Why else would she
come! It was funny, but not amusing; funny peculiar.
Her troubles had nothing to do with me. I was no
brother-confessor, if that was what she wanted. I was
not in that category. The category included 'objective
bystander'. It was annoying she could think such a
thing.

If she would only not visit me!

Why did she? I felt like screaming. Maybe she mis-
took me for a monk. That was her habit, not mine.

I was looking about for money. No damn money. My
God. But the kitchen sink. Yes, there by the draining
board. Where else. I was going mad. Oh well.

She was smiling. Good. But it was nice to see.

I was not apologizing for a damn thing. That includes
the draining board. Why! It was mine. Whose life was it!

Okay one can have less than positive habits. One of
mine was emptying my pockets where ere I happened
to be. When one empties one's damn pockets there are
sundry other objects, pieces of wool, old tissue with

cracked snotters and God knows what else. Dirty greasy coins. Where had that money been! Look at it! Dirty greasy coins! Do not let it near food, oh keep it away from the food. Especially fresh meat. My God the case for vegetarianism was strong.

But that was was not her. She never said that. Who the hell did say that?

My mother!

Interesting to have mixed Jennifer up with my mother, dear old mum.

But anyway, I would keep my money where I wanted. It was my bloody money. As also my apartment. Or studio. Nowadays it was a studio. Oh I am buying a studio, I am renting a studio. Everybody said it. Pretentious crap, as if everybody was an artist. I have a loft studio. A studio up in the loft. I need it for the light. That was these middle-class television programmes shot in New York City and featuring all these beautiful young people. A load of shit. In the old days a loft was the attic. Nowadays it was a penthouse suite. Old Mike Gilroy referred to it as a bedsit. We shared a first name. I was young Mike and he was old Mike. He was from Wales and worked in the storeroom. I worked in the office. He called me snooty but he was only kidding.

A bedsit was a bed-sitting-room. A room with a bed to sit in, a room you sit in that also has a bed. That was the studio, one single room where you had a bed and a sink and a chair, all crammed in together with a single wardrobe, a ward for your robes. If ever we wear robes we store them in this ward.

Ward!

One of these days it was the lock-up wing for me, I knew it, nothing more certain. How else to cope? How else!

The world was going crazy. Did dictionaries even exist any longer? That was old Mike's position. A typical old-timer. The world has gone to the dogs. Dogs. Was I a dog? I felt like a damn dog, especially with her around. No sex for ten years. What was that about, that was me, slight exaggerations here and there, thank God otherwise I would be out the window, I would have jumped out the window.

She was waiting for me by the outside door. She knew my habits. Mike, she said.

What?

We dont have to go out.

Yes we do, unless you dont want to.

I dont mind, I dont mind if we dont.

I shrugged, not looking at her. Because of course we had to go out. Because I was going mad and could not have coped with her presence, never! Not in isolation. I required the additional anxiety of other people, the life-saving force of other people.

How's Marianne? I said.

Oh, good, she's doing good.

School and all that?

Yeh, thanks for asking.

But the idea of not asking after her daughter! What did she think of me? That spoke volumes, it really did. Why had she even come!

Seriously, she might have phoned first. Why not? Did she think I never left the place! Like I had nowhere to go. Work and sleep. That was not the case, not at all. Why would she think it? Was I such a a – what? a wreck? she thought I was a wreck? Probably. Probably she did.

I followed her downstairs. There was a sense of – a definite sense of – of relief, yes sir, a sense of relief coming from her. It was like a draught of air! I felt it!

People take you by surprise. It is intentional. Then that is them, they have the advantage and will retain it until you retrieve it.

Society is a jousting match

But at least she agreed to come to a bar. A coffee house would have been a nightmare. A café or one of these damn what-do-you-call-thems central damn perks. I had forgotten what you even called the bloody places, people sat in them, and there was no beer and no damn spirits. Maybe you got wine. People went to them and were served cheesecake, lattés and liqueurs. You expected it to be full of these white horrors, chins all shaking, the plumply rich and fat wealthy, all eating their Stilton cheese, imported from the French Alps.

Then we were walking, and how we walked! Our elbows, wrists and coats touched, frequently they touched. My coat touched hers on the hem, mine touched hers. Could my coat be described simply as 'me'? 'I touched her' instead of 'my coat touched her.'

There were a couple of ordinary bars in the vicinity thank God, where your ears could relax and they knew how to deep-fry a sausage. The nearest was an ugly place and I disliked drinking there but no point walking miles when a return journey is all that lies ahead. I used to like walking but that was the problem, one had to come home. Sunday was my favourite day. The one day a body could drop money into a beggar's cup and remain sane. What could be better than the city on a Sunday? The evil horrors have returned to their country mansions and one can walk around at one's leisure.

At all other times I barely walked anywhere. How come? It was nothing to do with laziness, I was not a lazy man. Not in my own estimation. But I was honest. She could not have accused me of dishonesty. Never! Never never never!!!

Surely not. If so then things had changed; things had certainly changed. But people do change in this world. If one seeks certainty, if one were to seek one fixed truth, one by which we might construct a universe, then here is that one certainty, that one fixed truth: people change. Ha bloody ha.

I heard her shivering. My God. And the traffic was busy. How come it was so busy at lunchtime? She used to worry about a car losing control and crashing into the passersby. If I was late home from work! Yes! She used to worry about me. Oh hell, hell hell.

Or should one laugh; an hysterical outburst.

In the old days she would have walked closely by me. But would her arm have been in mine? Lovers entwine arms. Had she ever entwined mine? Or what about me? Had I ever done it to her, entwined? Was this a deficiency and if so who was to blame, if anyone, perhaps

no one; why do we always have to blame people, especially those closest to us, and she was, had been so, and
was looking older. God almighty! She really was. And
walking with her shoulders hunched, and head raised.
Head raised. This would cause physical problems in
later years. For the spine. Women develop spinal problems; bone conditions for heaven sake surely walking
properly was a help! Surely to God! Hey Jennifer, I
said.

What?

Oh nothing. Only watch the way you walk. You
know.

What?

You dont want a weakened spine.

What do you mean?

How you walk. I shrugged. That spondulitis thing or
whatever you call it, women get weak spines

Oh thanks, she said, thank you, thank you. She
paused in walking and smiled at me, and shook her
head, shook her head at me, and traffic passing everywhere, and people, all people, all sorts passing, the
whole damn world, all passing, and in front of me, with
her there and saying it to me. If I had been in my teens
I would have blushed.

She had to move sideways to avoid a boy on a skateboard, I also stepped to the side. If I had been that age I
would never have owned a skateboard. But why not?
You only have to be careful, I muttered.

She looked at me and we continued on. But it was not
a mean look or a chiding look, there was a sympathy

there. She thought I had been an overly protected boy, that my mother was a tyrant. My mother was not a tyrant. My plight had nothing to do with maternal so-to-speak mismanagement.

We hardly spoke another word on the walk but she did smile now and then, when she saw me watch her. And I did watch her. Okay. There were these large store-windows. It was quite embarrassing. You were both walking towards one and then looking into the reflection at the same moment. I pretended not to be doing it. I did not even care about my appearance. I had no ego. No ego! What in heaven's name did that mean? Ego me mihi meum: everybody has an ego. Well not me, not in that sense. I was a damn weed! A nine-stone weakling, thirty-six years of age and I only bloody hell my body, an embarrassment.

Who cares. Bodies are bodies. Then again
No.
But there was a demeaning side to what was happening. I could not take all the blame. Once upon a time ours was a proper relationship.

I have to describe myself in the third person.

At least they slept together, once upon a time. Once upon a time she enjoyed his company. Yes, for its own sake. When males and females sleep together it is a very fine thing indeed when they are also friends. Maybe not with bisexual males who are noted for their one-night stands and general promiscuity. Promiscuity. The word itself, the herald of untold mystery. He knew one fellow who drank in the same local bar as himself and acted in a coy manner. Mike was not unfriendly but distant; typically he was drunk by the end of the evening [a damnable lie!] and joked loudly with the barstaff. Two other fellows drank in this bar and might have been lovers in that non-physical masculine manner, they were forever kissing and canoodling. Bidding one another hail or farewell was an excuse to get physical.

Forget the third person: On one occasion I was in the bar for a quick beer on my way home from the office and I heard one of them saying, Dont give me a kiss.

This was in reference to a drink the one had bought for the other, so I assume the kiss would have been an expression of thanks.

Nobody can be friends with everybody, 'not even in California'. That was the title of a movie I saw recently. 'Not even in California'. Characters kept saying it all the time, it was one of these in-joke expressions the beautiful people have. But was it true or simply one more prejudice?

Life is full of prejudice. I didnt have many friends, bisexual or otherwise. Was that the result of prejudice? But you cannot be prejudiced against everybody. Or can you? Perhaps. There was a name for that? And was that name not 'misanthrope'? Was I a pathetic misanthrope? Well if I was I was. No damn wonder.

I could be honest about myself, to myself. Why conceal matters from one's inner psyche? That would have been foolish. Those of us lucky enough to have a psyche. Even an outer one. Do people have outer ones?

Jennifer knew I was better than that. If we cannot be honest with our own selves what chance has the world? I am talking survival. Less than none in my estimation. In bygone days she would have assumed that about me. Now I meant so little to her that – well, I was no longer treated as a male human being, a masculine human being, only an ordinary kind of – what? A man? Yes, an ordinary man, and an ordinary man can be anything if we are talking women. Women see a man as a man, and some more than that, as males. I was not too ambitious. This latter would have sufficed for me. But it was not to be. Not only was I an ex-boyfriend, I was an ex-male. Not only was I neutral, I was neutered. A neutered neutral, as far as she was concerned. Not only her, the entire world, or that part of society I was forced to find myself within. Within.

Within is an extraordinary concept. People would never understand how extraordinary a concept it is.

Jees, life was so horrible. It was high time I returned home. I was sick of this city. Even the geography or topography, whatever you call it, the layout. You never knew where you were; your bearings kept disappearing. *Where the hell am I?*

Seriously, where were the mountains? You never knew where you were because you could not see the mountains. There werent any mountains. No horizon. The horizon did not exist. A man could not be himself in this damn city. I should have gone home years ago. Instead I remained, I remained. And then I met her, the great misfortune. People have misfortunes and maladventures.

Malodorous maladventures. Mal is a fine word, if you are Spanish. Even if you are not, even for English-speaking men of colour. Men of colour! A person said this on television recently. I was what they appeared to be calling white so did that make me invisible? I too was a man of colour. Why did people not speak correctly, speak correctly.

Jennifer had stopped talking to me in an honest and true fashion. We had walked five blocks to reach the bar and she had yet to utter one single and solitary true and honest, honestly open word. Perhaps she was thinking of her wee girl. If she had been my daughter I would have worried constantly. Jennifer was a strong parent, stronger than I would have been. She might have been thinking of her daughter but not panicking, not in that anxious way.

She was simply not talking, not talking to me. Perhaps she had made a vow.

Not literally, obviously. Because she had spoken, she had replied to occasional comments. These boring details on the layout of the area we were walking. I am one of those boring bastards who point out local landmarks to people. They were not so boring, not in my estimation. The local politicos had outdone themselves in the past few months. One entire street had been sold to a huge supermarket chain and there were rumours that the sale of an adjoining street was pending. How could the politicians sell off a street? Yet they did. A few locals kicked up a fuss. The cops came in and removed the residents, whether at gunpoint or not, who knows. Hey! How can they do that?

They just did buster.

But that street belongs to the people of this community!

Oh yeh? Up against the wall anarchist mother-fucker!

The banks owned it. The banks owned the street. Oh well, that is capitalism. Now they were selling the adjoining street and no one batted an eyelid. That is the Earth for you. But who gave us the information? The local newspaper, radio and television stations. But who gave them the information?

Dont you want a supermarket?

Sure we do. This was a huge one. The adjoining street was for its satellites, two lesser supermarkets, one a giant liquor store and the other a pharmacy that specialized in hardware – some combination!

Jennifer always walked quickly. I had to touch her elbow to slow her down. We moved out of the way to avoid a schoolbus; wee children of about five years of age disembarked and near to them a troop of guys in hardhats. Look, I said, what a comparison! If I had a camera, that juxtaposition.

She smiled. You still like kids.

Pardon?

Jennifer smiled again, and shook her head.

But what a strange thing to say. I dont feel guilty about liking kids, I said, why should I?

They dont threaten.

No they dont threaten.

She smiled.

Why are you smiling?

Because if you had a kid of your own …

I'm thirty-six years of age Jenny, know what I mean, I should be a father. My sister is two years younger than me and she has four of them; four of them.

Mm.

I miss yours never mind nonexistent ones of my own.

She looked at me but said nothing. She didnt want to talk about this. Neither did I. She knew I was fond of her daughter. And likewise she was fond of my young sister for God sake if mine and Jennifer's relationship had depended on the existence of other relations we would have been married long since and I would indeed have been a father and not only a step-one and sure I missed all of that, but it was also to miss something I never had and therein lies madness. The child one never had. To hell with that.

And another schoolbus, we continued walking, and along a farther block before we turned off and along, and along again, to the bar, the bar.

We expect things to harmonize, I said, even in super-stores, but how the hell do they fit pharmaceuticals and hardware together? I mean it calls itself a pharmacy but the hardware is the main thing about it: I'll take a pair of scissors, three wood chisels, a pair of pliers, and a packet of headache powder thank you very much!

Jennifer grinned.

At least you arent patronizing me.

Yes.

Now you are.

You are always so critical.

It has nothing to do with critical. Streets, buildings and supermarkets, you forgot how boring I was.

She chuckled.

You sarcastic woman.

We arrived in the back alley where the bar was located. Oh I remember this one, she said, it hasnt changed much at all.

The outside entrance to the bar had a marble appearance but other than that was completely nondescript. Yet here she was examining it like it was a something or other a painting damn thing, a sculptured object from medieval Spain, which it was not, but then inside, inside the lobby! That was what she remembered. Of course! It was me that forgot. Oh, she cried, look at that, look!

I smiled.

My God!

I knew you would remember, I said although I was lying. She was pointing at the ceiling which had singularly shaped bricks and tiles that reminded strangers of a famous religious painting. Da Vinci's *Last Supper*! is what most of them cried. Us locals had to explain that it wasnt Da Vinci's *Last Supper*! but that of our Lord! The odd thing is that these strangers used to allow us the benefit of the doubt, as though we were authorities on religious art because we drank in that bar – and one has to choose one's words carefully; in other circumstances I would have said 'drank in that damn bar'.

Jennifer stood with her head craned, enjoying it. In fact I had forgotten the name of the painting, had actually forgotten its name, this most famous work of the Christian epoch.

Oh well, it was not my fault, how can we be blamed for our memory. For our lack of a memory. We do not blame a child for being born with one leg shorter than the other. Although this was slightly different; ageing bodily parts. I said, I'm thirty-six; the big three zero is history for me. The four zero next.

I held the door open for her, waiting; when she finished looking up and walked through I whispered to her: Jenny can I ask you something? What am I to you nowadays? What do I mean to you? Am I a sexless object? In all sincerity, is that how you see me?

She didnt reply. Yet I had spoken honestly. My only motivation was to discover the truth. That was it. Truth is what it was about. My only goal. What was its nature! A man might ask these things. It is an aid to self-discovery. Maybe we have been making mistakes. If so and someone informs us – e.g. erstwhile partners – then we can change, we can change and become better people, better citizens, better lovers, better patriots. People want to be better, I said, even me, I want to be better, not only a better patriot but a better human being.

Ssh.

Ssh?

She shook her head and was quiet.

What is it? I said.

Just be careful Mike.

Am I talking out of turn?

Yes.

Was I being sarcastic?

When? she said, and shook her head again; this time she closed her eyes! Dont let us talk about it now, she said but smiled. Get yourself a beer.

Yeh, I shall get myself a beer, and I shall drink myself a beer.

And I ordered an orange juice for her. The bartender was big. He was one of those guys with seventeen chins and seventeen bellies, each of which took it in turn to quiver. He was wary of me and didnt like my accent. So what? He poured the pint and I waited. He ducked below the counter for the orange juice. I wanted to ask if I could choose the oranges but he would have tossed me out the bar for insubordination. Instead I whistled a wee tune to myself.

I had been drinking in this bar for seven years! He made me feel like it was five minutes.

Never mind and relax, relax.

Whh whh whh, whh whh whh

[me whistling under my breath]

Jennifer had gone to a table at the side of the bar where I usually went. She didnt like standing at bars with me. I got the equivalent of road-rage.

At last I received the booze. She had taken off her coat when I arrived with the glasses. I noticed the yellow cardigan she was wearing. It was good quality. I nearly said classy. Or 'classic'. Jennifer was both classy and classic, a classy lassie. Some dame altogether. At one time she wore only grey and dark colours, navy blues and blacks. I like your cardigan, I said, it is nice.

Cardigan? She shook her head.

Is that not what it is? a cardigan?

She said nothing to that but for some reason appeared suspicious. Of me? How come! Now she looked away.

What the heck was wrong with 'cardigan'? My mum's description. And I think my sister used it too. Or was that the same thing!

I lifted my beer but didnt sip it, too predictable. She appeared not to be watching me but everything I did she noticed, I knew she noticed. Life was so damn complicated.

She was away looking at something else. I followed her gaze and who should it be but Mr and Mrs Duponzer, an older couple who lived farther down my street and, like myself, preferred to walk the miles to here rather than find somewhere more local.

Occasionally they trapped me into conversation. I got the feeling they were 'saving me from myself'. No doubt they mulled over my situation within the safety of their own fireside, whatever that might mean. People had long since stopped having firesides. City ordinances decreed otherwise.

City ordinances decreed. What kind of mumbo jumbo is that? My brains were sozzled. Not as an effect of alcohol but my years. In this culture thirty-six was Methuselah's nephew.

I could remember when I was nineteen. In those far-off days it was summer fifty-two weeks of the year. People did not speak of boyfriends and girlfriends, not back then, it was fiancés and marriage partners. People spent their life together. It was taken for granted. Working-class people, blue-collar communities. None of these invisible bourgeois bloodsuckers. Real people. That was Mr and Mrs Duponzer. They could not be separated. Even to imagine them separate, I could not do it. This was the kind of couple they were, this was their relationship.

So they still come in? she said.

I beg your pardon?

She smiled and shook her head like this was the real reason I had brought her here: to see an old married couple who still loved one another. My life amused her. I was glad. Yes well there they are, I said, there they are.

Bar meal?

That is correct, I said, what is wrong with a bar meal? I thought you would have approved. They do it a lot, the Duponzers. Other couples do it too. They come out together and do enjoyable togetherly things.

Oh Mike you are so defensive.

Am I?

Really.

Sorry about that.

Jennifer stared at me a moment, then smiled. You are.

Okay.

But you are. She chuckled. So defensive!

I'm not saying a word. I'm only glad I make you smile.

You do make me smile.

Yeh well I am pleased about that. I'm pleased.

I see that.

Look what does it matter whether I'm defensive or not? What does it matter? Mr and Mrs Duponzer enjoy their bar meals together. They do not do it everyday. Not as far as I know. Maybe if they've been out shopping together or taking in an early movie.

Do you mean an early morning screening?

Pardon? Do you want me to ask them?

If you like ... Jennifer was smiling again. Sarcasm is contagious

They go out together, I said, and they do things together. Then they come in here on their way home. Together. It is a natural thing.

Is it?

Sure. They do it a lot.

Excuse me? Jennifer was looking at me in that curious way, but it was me that was curious, a sort of 'curiosity'. That was how she saw me: a curiosity.

And where was the dignity in that? But probably I was a curiosity. Curiosity. The word wasnt even in my vocabulary. I would never have described a person as 'curious'. Especially not an ex-partner with whom one had been intimate. Only strangers are curious. Unless a behaviour had become so.

So that was it. My behaviour had *become* curious.

The behaviour of long-time intimates might change, might become 'curious'. I was an eccentric as far as she was concerned. Why not call a spade a spade, you think I'm an eccentric?

She smiled again. Her hand was to her mouth. There was a word for this. What the goddam hell was the word!

She reminded me of a salesman who thinks he has you cornered. What will he have you buy! You will buy something. But what? It is his choice. You have no escape. Not until he has finished enjoying himself at your expense.

This is the mistake salesmen make. They dangle you on their fishing rod and wont reel you in, like a cat with a mouse and to hell with metaphors. Once he toys with you your chance arrives.

They always become arrogant. Salesmen amuse me. They really do. I had been dealing with them for years. Their major psychological error is the search for applause, whether from you as customer-victim or one of their colleague-perpetrators. You see them grinning; cats at the cream jug.

We have all been salesmen at one time but generally we are not, generally we are the fish trapped in the net, preparing to be served on a plate. Now here was Jennifer. My God but it surprised me that she too, she too …

What is it? she said.

I didnt think you would remember the old Duponzers.

Are you serious! I'm not likely to forget them. She shook her head. She blinked at me. Why did she blink at me? Now she frowned. Frowned! They provided half our conversation, she said.

Oh well that's not fair, I said, that really is not fair.

She shrugged.

It isnt. I stared at her. I found her incredible. Each gesture she made, no matter how minuscule, was a question. Excluding words her language contained the widest vocabulary of anyone I ever met, including my father who was a scholar if not a gentleman. He was too, mean old bastard. But he never tired of learning; even on his deathbed. Bring me my Thesaurus! His favourite book. He had three of them. That was my legacy. Two were different editions of the same thing but the third was a wee old edition of Roget's Everyman, volume 1, 2 or 3.

Jennifer had a wider vocabulary than my father and it all stemmed from the body. Words had nothing to do with it. Every last move was a comment, each part of her body, everything, from fingers to toes, every indice a sentence, a statement. If she wiggled an ear I was obliged to answer: What am I to do? What do you ask of me? What is it you want!

Which is what I had never discovered.

But what did I want of her? She said I was the most suspicious man she ever had known. She meant 'slept with'. She always slept with her boyfriends. From girlhood upwards. She experimented. She told me herself. I hated it. I wish she hadnt but she had. Oral sex too. I hated it, hated it. Not the act but just, my God, why did she tell me? I did not want to hear about it, none of that stuff, I didnt want to know about those guys.

I imagined them laughing. Macho shits, drooling over their beer.

Jennifer went her own way. She always did. That was that. That was indeed that. If she had been male she would have been into science; something I was never into myself.

I pointed at the Duponzers and then to the big sign at the corner of the bar. See that, I said, they go shopping together and they eat bar meals together. They do meal-deals if you havent noticed, they give you membership cards, you buy three beers and they give you a bowl of chips and a slice of pizza; another beer and you get these onion things in batter. There is nothing wrong in that. I dont think so anyway. Maybe other people do. If other people think so, well then, they are entitled to their opinion, whatever it is. Even sex, why do we think things about older people?

Ssh.

But it is true.

Yeh but be quieter.

Okay but if they perform sex acts together. Why not? If they are older, so what?

Ssh.

Okay, I whispered, but surely you would not deny it to the elderly?

Dont be ridiculous.

It isnt to do with ridiculous, it is natural, human nature. It is a normal need, an everyday part of our life. Even homely, if we think of it in this sense, sex is homely.

Jennifer grinned.

This caught me off guard. What I said was stupid. At the same time, you find it funny, I said, but it's true. Sex is an ordinary everyday experience, every bit as natural as eating or drinking so this is why I said what I did because to me it is homely. Sorry but that is what I think and I am not going to retract it. You are two years younger than me, ergo thirty-four.

Thirty-three.

Thirty-three? Yeh …

She smiled.

It's your birthday next month.

Dont remind me.

Imagine forgetting your birthday!

Oh Mike.

I'm being serious.

Dont be silly. Anyway, you didnt, you just said it.

Right … But I had forgotten. I lifted my beer and sipped at it – for only the second time since our arrival. She put me on guard, praise the Lord.

There was something in her smile that complemented the yellow cardigan. Since the split she had transformed into another being. I thought it unfair. There was a lack of justice in the world that rendered major questions meaningless. 'Transform' was not the word, and not 'transmogrified' either.

Blossom! She had blossomed! She had blossomed into a sort of

What! A flower? What a total and absolute half-baker of a cliché. I felt like roaring in laughter. A flower! Oh pretty little petal. Imagine I said it to her, pretty little petal! My leetle chickadee! I was a wreck. Maybe I was having a breakdown. Not emotional but mental. Intellectual. I had failed to recognize it. Because it was happening to me and not someone else. She would recognize it. She knew me. She was the very person that could tell if I was really me, rather than a mad variation! Am I a mad variation of myself?

What are you smiling about? she said.

Pardon?

You were smiling.

Was I?

You were.

Only being with you I suppose, it is so damn difficult.

Huh?

It is. You dont think of that.

Yes I do.

You dont.

Oh of course I do.

If you did you would have stopped visiting me. You would have stopped visiting me months ago.

She was smiling. I smiled back at her. I had to. Because what else.

And why was she smiling. Because I was predictable. Because she did not believe me. She did not believe I thought what I thought. Now she shook her head. But at the table; not at me, she did not shake her head at me. That would have been playful and she was not being playful. The playful days had gone. Now she avoided looking at me. I was going mad. I had this sensation I had spoken aloud. Did I speak aloud? I must have spoken aloud. Otherwise

From the moment we sat down at this table. I saw it now. She was avoiding eye-contact.

Because eye-contact was the very breath, the very breath. She took pleasure in such contact, even in exaggerated forms such as staring people down. It was a game she and her daughter played, and mummy always won.

So she would not look at me. After what we had endured. Which was sad, that surely was sad. Oh but I wished, I wished ...

She was smiling.

Why are you smiling?

I thought you were going to ask if I wanted a drink.

Pardon?

The way you looked at me, I thought you were about to ask if I wanted a drink.

But I bought you a drink.

Yes I know.

I pointed to her orange juice which was untouched. Would you like a gin or something?

No.

Are you sure? A Cointreau?

It is two o'clock in the afternoon. Anyway, I dont drink much alcohol, only the odd occasion.

Could there be a more odd occasion than this, I wondered, but not aloud.

I was close to abstinent myself nowadays so it was a surprise she should refer to alcohol in that manner, as though I were an habitual drinker. I was never one. I knew habitual drinkers and knew their habits; enough to know about myself. We see ourselves in others and I did not see myself when I looked at them. Maybe she mixed me up with someone else, one of her other menfriends.

'Menfriends' was the word, they certainly werent boyfriends. Jennifer had men. So many I confused identities. Like she had confused me. It beat everything. Finally I knew where I came on the scale of things. So then she talked to me like she now was doing, as though I was a brother-confessor or some damn asexual jackass.

She spoke about them to me. She actually did that. I let her do it. I even expected it. I knew why she saw me and here it was again afuckinggain, seeing this married guy who lived apart from his wife and family. This is who she was seeing. God almighty. But it sounded complicated. She denied it was complicated. She attempted an explanation of why it was not complicated, why it was so uncomplicated, all of its uncomplicatedness. She was telling me! Why are you telling me, I said, I dont want to know, I'm not a brother-confessor for God sake a what-do-you-call-it, an objective bystander, some kind of monk.

Ssh. You are talking too loud.

I shook my head.

You always talk too loud. You do. I wish you would be less … If you would speak more quietly. You arc too loud. Honestly Mike, you are. Really. I wish you would be more calm.

I looked at her.

Can you be? Please.

Okay, I said, but no wonder, hearing about your life, when you start telling me stuff it is so damn complicated it drives one absolutely bloody bananas. It is a complete hotchpotch.

If you dont speak more quietly I am leaving.

What?

Honestly now dont do it Mike, people can hear.

She was looking across to the bar. But the people there waited to be served. They were not eavesdropping. Only interested in their own order, what they were getting to drink and if somebody was going to be served before them, if they came first into the bar and someone coming behind them was served first before them. That could happen in this bar with mister seventeen bellies, it drove you insane. The bartenders here were not the worst but occasionally they ignored individuals out of spite. Nothing more nothing less. If you were the ignored individual it was tough luck. Except if you were new to the culture and neglected to tip. Oh my God what a criminal way to behave, the asshole dont tip. So people do not serve them! That was the mentality in this bar. I could get nauseated by the place. Why did I continue coming? There are perennial questions; that was one.

Some of the faces were familiar. I noticed them nod to the Duponzers and one of them even gave me a wave. He was in here most days of the week. An unhappily married guy. One time we spoke together and all he did was gossip and bitch, that was all he did. People squabbled. Over the pettiest of matters. If too many strangers were present they pretended things were friendly but they were not. As soon as a stranger became a regular he got drawn in too. Not just hes, they were shes. This was a bar where women could drink alone.

It was all meaningless crap. I hated it. Even when Jennifer and I were together. We treated it as a joke. Mr and Mrs Duponzer. One of those old European names now Anglicized. It sounded French and looked Dutch, maybe Belgian. I once asked them in a fit of boredom. They did not know. Mr Duponzer did not care. He only laughed. His wife did the talking. She thought it was an English name but maybe not, what did it matter.

People here didnt care about such stuff. If there were positive aspects to this bar then that was one. Issues around race and ethnicity were irrelevant. Generational gaps were different. I was one of the youngest regulars and was patronized accordingly. Which was interesting in reference to Jennifer. This married guy she was seeing, he was still married. Him and his wife lived in separate abodes during the week but under the same roof every weekend! For the sake of the kids.

Oh yeah. I cleared my throat when she said that, reached for the beer. Why did she fall for such crap? For the sake of the family, the collective unit. Whatever that was supposed to mean. In my experience families were not collective units, more like disparate noumena. Collective units is a joke.

Only for some, she said. Perhaps for you.

Mm, I said, and nothing further. This asshole went round and stayed with his wife and family every single weekend. He never returned to his own place until Monday evening, after work. Every Sunday morning they went bowling together, on Saturday evenings they had trips to the movies, they went to the park. All of it. They even went swimming to a members-only swimming club.

Her as well, I said, his wife?

His wife what?

She goes on these bowling and swimming trips?

I suppose.

Do you share his weekday home?

No. Although I could: if I wanted.

Has he asked you?

The option is there.

So he has asked you?

The option is there.

Mm. I nodded.

What?

Nothing.

So why are you saying mm and nodding your head in that manner?

What manner?

I said to you that the option is there and it is there.

Fine.

The two of us prefer it that way. It might sound incredible to you, sorry. But it's common in other social circles.

That people have two homes?

Sometimes.

Jennifer that isnt social circles it's economic circles. If what you're saying is true then I wouldnt trust this guy as far as I could throw him.

Nobody is asking you to trust him.

It is garbage.

To you maybe. Other people dont see it that way.

If he is seeing his wife every weekend and then seeing you through the week, at his convenience, because at other times he is completely free, because you have your own place as well, so he can do whatever he likes, so I mean I dont know, he only just I dont know – except

What …?

I dont trust him, and would never trust him, not in a month of Sundays. You know what I'm talking about.

No Mike sorry, I dont.

Come on.

Come on what?

It's obvious.

What's obvious?

How do you know he doesnt have another girlfriend? I shrugged. Another two girlfriends? Three. Know what I mean, you're talking transmitted diseascs here.

Dont be revolting.

She gazed around to see if anybody was listening. Mr and Mrs Duponzer were staring into space. She shook her head. I cannot believe you, you are so horrible.

Well I'm not trying to be horrible I mean for God sake, does he wear condoms?

I beg your pardon!

I whispered, You are too trusting. That's you all over just trusting people all the time, you always trust them.

I'm not discussing this with you.

Yes you are Jenny that's exactly what you are doing. That's why you came and dragged me out the house.

She stared at the untouched orange crap.

At least be honest about it. You are too trusting. Apart from where I'm concerned. You trust everybody except me, you believe everybody except me. And I'm the one, I'm the one …

I stopped. Because there was no point. And my head, my head was just – enough. Was there ever such a being as a weak woman? It was a figment of the collective male imagination.

She grinned.

How come? Because I was smiling, because I was remembering something, stupid goddam cat.

What is it? she said.

That old fucking stupid saucer!

The cat's?

Yeah. I gave you it for an ashtray and the cat licked it poor bastard.

If you prefer me not to smoke then I wont.

I'm not saying that.

Jennifer nodded, she was holding a pack of cigarettes. Do they still have the non-smoking section?

Every bar has a non-smoking section. Outside the door.

Thanks.

Sorry.

Nowadays they dont want you smoking at the door.

I dont want you smoking at all, but so what, it's personal. If you've got to do it you've got to do it. I'm not going to make it hard for you. If you want to step outside the door I shall accompany you, be it hailing or raining or whatever the hell.

She had a cigarette halfway out the packet.

You are a member of the public, I said, so you do have certain entitlements, certain prerogatives. It's obviously a surprise seeing you smoke again because you did so well beating the habit in the first place.

Obviously?

Obviously?

You said obviously.

Because it is a surprise. I admired you so much for stopping. I'm talking in the first place, you showed fine determination

It wasnt in the first place, I smoked in the first place.

Nobody smokes in the first place.

My mother and father both smoked. So it was in me from birth, pre-birth. My mother and father were nicotine addicts. Why are you frowning?

I'm not frowning I just, I dont believe you.

But it is true, whether you believe me or not. They gave my mother an ashtray in the delivery room.

That is nonsense.

Jennifer smiled.

Honestly?

Yeh.

What was it a private hospital?

Of course.

I knew your parents were stinking rich. You only pretended they werent.

She chuckled – a laugh more, a quiet laugh, a beautiful laugh. I was expecting her to say something more but she was not, she was not being trapped into it. Never. Never never never.

How come I ever had her as a girlfriend in the first place! She was way way beyond me! Way way beyond! She was just

something. Something else. She was watching me. Sorry.

What?

I do apologize.

For what?

I looked at her when she asked that. Really, it was some question. For what! For smiling, I said, it is just so goddam fucking ironic.

I know.

You know? Yeh, of course you do. Let me tell you something; I felt good this morning. When I woke up, I felt good. Now a massive great shadow is hovering above me. It is you that's brought it. You've created it. I'm talking about you, your presence.

She held the unlit cigarette between the fore and middle fingers of her right hand. Then she winked.

Yes I tried to smile, I did, I failed. I sniffed slightly and drank a little beer. I realized about the wink, why she had winked at me. She had caught me in the act of staring at her. I was staring at her. That was why she winked.

Lines from old movies. Damn you woman! I should have been wearing a Noël Coward smoking-jacket. Damn you woman! James Mason. Damn you woman! She would be in the long black dress, those black silk gloves that come up to the elbow and all wrinkles but intentional wrinkles: silk. And her elbows, her shoulders, and her neck.

Former intimacies. Her body.

I could have thought more things. These were pressing my mind. Memories so solid they were physical. Yes I had been staring. I carried on staring. Simply the fall of her breasts. Once upon a time I would have blushed, the blood coursing, tugging the bra below, my tongue to the nipple. Had she forgotten!

All of it.

How familiar I was with her body. She must have forgotten. I had no sympathy for her and that is the God's truth. None at all. I wished it were untrue because I did feel for her, something for her. It was undeniable. If I could have been more sympathetic I would have been, but I could not.

Nothing could be done about that.

How had we ever managed to be intimate! Seriously intimate. Yet we had. Not only sex. Sure we had sex, of course we had. Her beautiful body, and mine – my whatever one calls it, body, mess of a body, my body, the inexpressible. Men's bodies are not so good.

One of life's sour mysteries.

Women and bodies. Sometimes I gazed at myself in the mirror when I was naked. A gaze is a vacant look. One sees nothing in particular, general traits and appearances. I was all misshapen. My testicles were the strangest-looking objects. My knees and thighs were so thin. Too thin. No woman could fall for me.

Nor had she fallen for me. It was me, I had fallen for her. I won her. I went after her, I broke her down. Everywhere she looked I was there till finally she caved in. Oh if I say yes maybe he'll go away! That was what she thought. She said yes to get rid of me.

Then I lost her.

Yet she wouldnt have been here unless she needed me. Surely not? Why else? I have to ask, I have to ask, why you're here and telling me all this? You knew I wouldnt be sympathetic. How could I be? These married men bastards, they're out-and-out – well, that is what they are, bastards, not to put too fine a point on it. Cant they just leave people alone?

She smiled.

It is not me that is naive, I said, it is you. That is the trouble. You think you are smart but you arent, not really.

She shook her head.

Face the fact, it wasnt you made the first move with this guy. You might think it but you did not. You are kidding yourself about that. It was him. Guaranteed.

She sighed, glanced towards the door.

I'm telling you how it was Jenny. He put himself in your way. He made sure you were aware of him. You would not have made the move if he hadnt set it up. I'm not saying he forced you against your will; what I'm saying is it would not have happened unless he allowed it, it was him made the running. There is a word for that, and I cant think of it. But it has to do with psychological, it is psychological.

A word for psychological?

Excuse me?

Sorry, she said, but is it a word for psychological you're looking for?

I'm not looking for anything.

Oh, I thought you were.

Well I'm not.

Sorry.

Was she being sarcastic? How could she have said that? Not to me! Surely not. Now she was smiling. I might have predicted it. Such a strange phenomenon. She had that ability to smile her way out of trouble. Women do. Not only women. Mainly women. And politicians. Smile smile smile. It was a sickening spectacle.

You asked me for another word for psychological, said Jenny.

Oh I did?

Dont be angry with me.

I'm not.

You are.

Never.

She sighed.

But dont act like I havent got an interest, that's all. You hurt me when you broke it off between us. Because you did not find me sexually attractive dont assume it was mutual.

I did find you sexually attractive. I did. I did find you sexually attractive.

There's no point saying that.

I did.

Dont say it if it's not true.

Oh Mike, you have such a low opinion of yourself. You do. Eventually it rubs off on people.

Oh does it?

You dont want me to say it because you dont want to know it. You dont want to believe it. You dont want to hear the truth. Sorry, but you dont. I wish you would stop doing it to yourself; there are too many martyrs in this world.

I smiled. She ignored it, she continued: It's all right being a martyr if people know. But why do it in secrecy, it'll only make you bitter; you are bitter anyway, you dont need other factors to help it along.

Mm.

Yes. She nodded.

I finished my beer. Her orange juice lay untouched. I pointed at it. I asked if you wanted a different drink earlier on, I said, I was talking about tea or coffee, not alcohol.

I beg your pardon?

I was not talking about alcohol.

Yes you were.

I wasnt

You said gin.

I didnt at all say gin.

You did.

I didnt.

Sorry but you did.

I didnt.

You did.

Well I dont remember saying it.

Well sorry but you did.

Do you want a cup of tea?

Tea? Will they do that for you?

They'll do it for anybody.

They'll do it for you because you're a good customer. What kind of tea do they have?

Any kind. Ordinary tea. What is it you're looking for, lemon green tea with a peppermint twist or something, frogs' legs and mint julep and burdock dandelions or some damn thing, vanilla with fudge flavouring, or one brought from the heights of the Andes mountains! Will I run round to the deli and get you a pack of special-flavoured tea-bags?

She smiled. I also smiled. I saw her hand now on the table and imagined it reaching to mine in that meas-ured way she had.

I thought you might have changed, she said,

Jees, you really know how to hurt people!

That is what I am talking about. You are so sarcastic.

I nodded.

So sarcastic. You are.

What can I say? Do you not think the very act of com-ing to tell me your troubles is sarcastic? I mean if that is not sarcastic I dont know what is, coming to my place like that, my home, and knowing what I'll do is anything, anything, I'll do anything, just whatever. Whatever. God, life is so fucking horrible fucking crap Jenny, so crap.

She could never have believed how much crap, never never, only just the worst, how life takes charge, takes a grip, and Jenny had a napkin in her hand. She was twisting it, looking at me. It was like a wetness about her eyes, dabbing the napkin there. Did I make her feel that way? No, it was mister married bastard.

Is that guy really hurting you? I said. Eh? Jees oh Jenny dont let him get you like that, a guy like him, it's not like you to let that happen. It really is not like you, know what I mean, a fucking shit like that, goddam rat.

She shook her head. I reached to touch her on the shoulder. She moved her shoulder slightly. He isnt a rat, she said.

Of course he is. Otherwise you wouldnt be here at all, never mind

Are you crying? You're not crying are you? Are you crying?

She shook her head. She didnt knock my hand from her shoulder. I left it there. Then she got up to go for a smoke. I went to the bar. Thirty-eight bellies waited. I saw your empty glass, he said, I wondered how long!

I smiled. He also smiled. I asked for two teas.

Teas?

Okay?

Sure.

One with milk and sugar and the other without, un solo.

I got some cookies, you want some cookies? English digestives.

Great, that's exactly it. Could I have a brandy as well please, and a glass of water on the side.

With ice?

I shrugged. Brandy was a good afternoon drink in my opinion. Neither one thing nor the other. It would go down well today. When I got the brandy I returned to the table. He would bring across the teas. Mr and Mrs Duponzer were looking across. I exchanged waves with them. They were a good old couple. So what if they were nosy? People were entitled to be nosy.

Anyway, they werent all that nosy. I have known nosier.

And what else is life? Life is nosy, nosiness. Everybody is nosy. I sat down. I felt very relaxed although she could have gone for good. If she had, okay, if not, still okay. Life was like that, okay, an okay life. Soon enough the big guy brought us the teas and the English digestives. It was a time for English digestives. They lay on a small plate next to the jug of milk and bowl of sugar. Better than okay. Thanks man, I said, that is it.

Later Jenny returned. I could smell the smoke. When she was seated she smiled at the tea and so forth. I proffered the small plate: Have an English digestive.

She grinned.

Go ahead, I said and could not stop smiling. That was big fucking thirty-nine bellies. What a wonderful goddam bartender!

Jenny lifted one and bit into it, nudged a crumb from the corner of her mouth. She saw me watching. Tasty, she said and chuckled.

English digestives are no laughing matter. And tell me this, I said, while we're on the subject, how come you are now the sort of woman who dons a yellow cardigan to visit her ex-lover, sharer of your bed and all the passions, and so on and so forth?

Jenny smiled.

Do you realize I get erections just taking part in this sort of what-do-you-call-it, conversation?

Ssh.

I do.

Dont say that.

But I do. Jenny …

Dont say it.

I stopped, I had been smiling but no longer. I saw the wetness round her eyes again and wanted to kiss them, only on her eyelids, where the fragility

Oh no, I said, you're going to make me cry.

Her head was bowed.

You are. Because here am I but it is him your tears are for. You're crying over him and here you are with me.

When I said this last she was blowing her nose into the napkin. I dreaded looking at her.

No I didnt.

Man to Man

That guy eh – what d'ye call him, I can never remember his name. He was giving her a row right in the middle of the floor. Ranting and raving. Her sitting there with the head bowed, maybe embarrassed or what, I dont know, ashamed maybe. She knew folk there and they were hearing it all. How come they were letting it happen, all just standing there? No just the barstaff. Everybody. Me too, I was one of them, what I mean, cowards, we were just I suppose well cowards really, we were cowards. So yeh, ashamed, she must have been.

But I felt like getting a grip of him, know what I mean, dirty bastard. But the best one to do it was another woman. See if she had done it! That really would have been the best. But there was nay other woman there.

There were women but no for that, taking on a guy like him I mean, fucking hell, ye wouldnay want to take on him. No even the likes of – well, no me anyway. Naw, I wouldnay.

Unless just batter him with something, that is what ye would have to do. Dont wait. Pick up something. Fucking heavy ashtray or what. A chair man know what I mean, a solid effort, fucking hit him with it.

On and on he went jesus christ and my hand started shaking. I was holding my pint, and so tight man gripping it, I had to let go. Breaking the glass, know what I mean, we're stronger than we think.

Dont tell me he is gony hit her, dont tell me. That is what I was thinking. Because if he hit her man see if he hit her ...

I shut my eyes.

Then guys near me, I heard them talking, about the Celtic and Hearts game. What was it a draw or some fucking thing, a disputed penalty? They were talking loud, loud. No just to drown out the angry guy's ranting. It wasnay just that.

What it was, to make it seem like it didnay mean nothing, no anything special. It was normal behaviour.

I noticed that before about guys, how when something awful was happening they started talking. Even just the telly, Ulster or Palestine or what, Iraq. Away they go about the football. Oh aye Celtic's got a hard game on Saturday, Rangers have it easy, what about the Liverpool game. Meanwhile it is carnage. No everybody. Some watch or else dont watch. Maybe they listen.

And it all goes on roundabout. Ye cannay shut up yer ears.

Dreams and hallucinations. I even get them when I'm sitting myself. Other folk will be the same although I havenay asked anybody, no even the wife. If I said it to her she would tell me to stop talking shite – well, rubbish; she doesnay swear, no that shite is swearing.

But fair enough, ye dont want to end up a babbler. Ye see these poor auld sods. In the pub they sit out the road. People leave them alone. They babble away to themself like somebody else is there and taking part in the conversation.

Well in a way there is somebody else. Them. They talk to themself as if they are another person, an actual other person. So there they are. So fair enough, one equals two; two parts make a whole and ye cant have the one and not the other. So then they give the answers to their own questions.

We all do that. But inside wur own head. That is the difference. Imagine we done it out loud! The guys in the white coats would come and take us away ha ha. Senile, an advanced case. Or just plain ordinary mad.

Human beings are near the surface. Just scratch and that is us.

Ranting and raving. It was excruciating, it really was. Ye felt like stuffing up the ears. I was gripping that pint of mine, so tight, jesus, needing to quell the thoughts quell the thoughts and all that racket going on it drove ye fucking nuts man it drove ye fucking nuts, that male-female fandango.

All kinds of mental stuff happens when ye are in for a pint. Couples! Hoh, fuck. I swallowed a mouthful of beer, keeping my face fixed. But no for long no for long and I was like Aw for fuck sake, landing my pint on the bar and pushing clear to the fresh air.

Ohhh man yeh.

That dampness in the air. I was so glad of that. I breathed deep, really deep. I imagined it all misty and ye were out in the country. Farms and fields. Aw aye. Even the way mist comes down ower the Clyde.

It does. The Clyde is country too, ye forget that.

And what about when ye look up and it is all grey patches of mist and through them ye see the night sky, maybe even the stars? I like that too.

Now was the sound of boys, teenage little cunts, that hee-haw voice they have, gon up and down. But cheery. Probably they were scouting about for lassies. Little did they know the lassies would be scouting about for them. Great to be young! Hoh! and I dont think, I was glad to be gon hame.

The Gate

I paid them the money and hoisted the bicycle onto my left shoulder, set off down the path. Quite an awkward path. The ground seemed very knotty; I worried about stubbing my toes and tripping. Nor could I see down properly. Owing to the bicycle my actual vision was obscured. On the other hand a natural deterioration takes place in the body and the eyes are not excluded from this. I understand that my sight fails but have been less aware of it in practice than some have predicted. My wife as an obvious factor. Christine, ah Christine.

My feet retain their sensitivity; along the path I was conscious of the twisted roots and branches. Also occasional slates, roof slates; I heard them fracture under my heels. Many were broken before I went trampling across. It was unavoidable. I wondered if the slates had been placed there by intention: broken pieces would embed in the earth between the roots, making the passage easier. It was reassuring to think this the case.

All in all a difficult terrain. I found it so anyway. The shrubbery itself was overgrown, if one could call it shrubbery. I say 'shrubbery': one might call it vegetation. In our marriage my wife was the gardener. Always, even if I could garden she was the gardener, and if one senses an antagonism one is not misguided.

It was thick and became thicker, this vegetation; a density. Manoeuvring became hazardous. One had to avoid shoulder-height obstacles such as branches and those jaggy, long-stemmed entities. I recollect them from childhood, horrible things that stabbed one's limbs. I was colliding and having to force a way through, and then also what felt like mesh, and perhaps was mesh, or meshes, shuddering – cobwebs! of course – I felt them across my head, the scalp and what remains of my hair, a sort of wafting touch, a dragged thread, scaly thin indices, skeletal. None of those exaggerations amused me. I termed them 'observations', tempered by the bicycle frame cutting into my shoulder.

On my initial entry into the garden I failed to notice how awkward it was along the pathway. I must have been sleepwalking. My head was so full of the potential bargain, the bicycle itself which I wanted for my grandson. He needed a bike and his birthday approached. Children need bikes. Children are expensive. Bicycles, I meant to say, are expensive.

Some received and some did not. Mine did not. Eventually they would, they too, they would, they would get one.

I would surprise the family with my purchase. It is true that I wanted to win my grandson's affection. My son-in-law was a difficult young man. If truth be told he was an awkward bugger. I believe that intellectually he was not my equal but in terms of cunning was, and of decision-making. He was forthright too. That annoyed me. One might praise forthrightness as a quality but only in those whose actions are tempered by good sense. I would never have accused my son-in-law of sense, certainly not of the worthy variety. My grandson favoured him, over myself, which is entirely normal. Fathers and grandfathers are not in competition. If only he might have remembered that.

My daughter was sympathetic but finally had made her bed. I did not begrudge her this. This world offers limited potential; one takes where one can. She told me she loved him. I found it excruciating.

I dare say her chosen partner would have found me difficult. Outwith the presence of a third party we did not communicate. My grandson offered that possibility. He was a cheery boy; he and I seemed to hit it off.

On the whole I thought it better to skip a generation and make my peace with my children's children. Christine and I found it too disagreeable for discussion. She lacked patience. In earlier times it was the root cause of our problems. Now she refused to discuss the situation which was ironic, given that the problems themselves had disappeared. Through age I imagine. Nevertheless, it was an unpleasant situation. Occasionally I yearned for earlier times, older times, when she and I fought like cat and dog, but later came together, as lovers often do. Nowadays her impatience overwhelmed me. Always it was directed against myself. Why was that? This morning I had seen the advertisement in the morning newspaper but when I read it out she would not listen. She refused to discuss 'the matter'.

I replied, It is not 'a matter' it is a bicycle. I wish to acquire a bicycle for our grandson. What is wrong in that? Is there something wrong in that?

No.

Well then?

I refuse to discuss it with you.

On second thoughts thank God, thank God. It was heartfelt! I had nothing to discuss with her. The relationship between myself and my son-in-law was not a subject for discussion.

Anyway, I would not describe it as a relationship. Arrogant bugger. Astonishing, that he could have considered himself the equal

The bicycle cut into my shoulder. Perhaps it was not a good bicycle. Good ones were lightweight. Or used to be. Nowadays – well, nowadays. Statements that begin in such fashion denote age, and anti-social odours.

The atmosphere in the garden seemed to have altered. It was almost peculiar. Certainly it was chilly. Once again I had been fooled by weather forecasters. I was wearing only a tee-shirt, a thin tee-shirt at that. Of course all tee-shirts are thin. I was not foolish. Elderly yes foolish no, at least not by nature. Nor by inclination, through the nurturing process, part and parcel of ageing.

It is true that I was a grandfather and this bicycle had been purchased for my grandson, a boy that I liked. I could imagine a grandson whom I did not like. I had two granddaughters also, by my son. Of course I liked them. Obviously I loved them. But in like fashion? Perhaps, given that we saw them so rarely. Difficult terrain altogether, gender and one's response. Absence makes the heart grow fonder. Perhaps, but proximity and habit bring greater rewards.

It was entirely possible, in fact probable, that my grandson would not want the bike. He held his own opinions, personal opinions. He was seven years of age but most independent. In this day and age such sensibility was crucial not simply for personal but for social development. The key to survival lay in communality. The present generation of adults neglected this.

Salutary, that my granddaughters would not have wanted the bicycle, had they been here to receive it. Nothing I acquired for them was treated seriously. They allowed me to tickle them and give them money. I occupied that typical elderly-male role; the ridiculous figure of fun, undiagnosed victim to early dementia. I only suffered the deteriorating condition: the rest of the family were its victims. Oh God.

But I needed to pause a moment. The damn bike. A certain discomfort, a certain – pain, I was experiencing pain, effected by the cycle frame, the crossbar itself, it seemed so heavy, or awkward somehow because how could it be so heavy, not so heavy. That was the stuff of delusion. Surely?

The path along towards the foot of the garden was steep, it became so. I had failed to notice this, that it was happening, that such a thing might conceivably happen at all. Until suddenly, suddenly. The unpredictable. What is 'the unpredictable'? Can God move in unpredictable ways? Are the limits of thought bound by man's own being? Could I be held responsible? Might I be considered

Nor had I noticed on the way up. I had not noticed on the way up! Oh well. My head was full. Full! he shrieked, full.

Foolish.

Dusk.

God rest ye merry gentlemen.

The path was hill-like. So damn awkward to negotiate because of the damn bushes, the general vegetation all overgrown, over growing, so-called shrubbery. One saw such bushes in the knowledge that as one looked the denser it became, their accursed life continuing unabated, fraction by fraction, oh yes they were growing, they would not stop growing.

Melodrama was a tendency of mine. Christine saw it in me and despised it. Rightly. I agreed with her. She said she did not despise it, but she did, obviously she did. Such tendencies are despicable, in this day and age, and occasionally I appeared powerless to halt that one. Things do crowd in on one; emotionally, intellectually, and in the outside world actual substances, material matter, it impinges. One cannot be separate.

Some branches were brambles and shooting out in my face. Bramble shoots. And I was having to dodge them, stepping from the path on to the earth where clumps of massive rhubarb grew in a row. Gigantic rhubarb. Onto the earth. Others could have said 'into'. To step into the earth. Ghastly thought.

Does dusk fall?

Dusk falling.

But if we insist on precision; for those of us who do. But why bother. Christine ridiculed precision, in me at any rate. Nowadays she did. In the early years it was that selfsame precision, my ability to prise out the truth. Wheedling the truth, she said. Wheedling. It was meant unkindly. In her opinion I only made matters worse. Obscurum per obscurius. I was guilty.

And would be dead soon enough, thank God.

A younger man might have jumped onto the bicycle and pedalled to freedom. A boy would have done so. A boy sees no risks. One places the bicycle on the ground, one jumps aboard, one pedals. Girl or boy. My daughter and my granddaughters. Or girls.

I wondered if the owners of the house watched me from the window. Who in heaven's name were they anyway. I wanted nothing to do with such people and resented that the purchase of this bicycle had forced the acquaintance. Economics is a loathsome matter. The man had been pleasant enough; although perfunctory is a more apposite term. The woman was downright hostile. I tried speaking their language. She interrupted at once with a carefully nuanced sigh. If she had been my wife 'good cause' would have been mine, for annoyance of a reasonable nature.

I recognized her sigh: only women are capable of such – such – emissions. Downright bad manners I called it. Rudeness is rudeness.

And the language of these people I found demanding. And when they do not help! The man was all right but she was not, she was scornful. Luckily for her Christine had not been present.

My wife's patience was limited, very limited. Neither was she fond of strangers. It caused friction between us when I so charged her. Life is difficult enough.

Yes, she said.

It is us; we are the strangers.

Thank you for the explanation. I can rely on you.

Sarcasm and Christine he sighed, wearily, wearily.

Damn weight. A dead weight. Bikes nowadays. It certainly was not light and yes, it was very awkward because of the chain and its protective metal guard, getting in my way, they just kept getting in my way thus having to carry the damn thing slightly out from my shoulder, I had to, thus unable to put all my strength behind it, I could not, so that too, my God, this was causing the problem and that tweaking tweaking, as though a tautness, as of a tendon coming to snap: that was the tweaking.

The thought of the trek home.

He sighed, sighed.

Of course the pedals were in the old design, which my grandson no doubt, no doubt, would find offputting. Only a fool expected gratitude.

Nothing was ever easy, arrived easily.

I could hardly walk here. But who could? The path was beyond discussion.

The gate at last. I saw it. Why not? Gates exist. The one entity whose existence one can rely upon safely. Where humankind existeth so too doth the gate, the gate.

But so relieved to find it! I was. Not until then did I realize the extent of that relief. Oh Christine. Almost I had been lost, lost! He who is lost now art found, along the garden path, up the garden path and down the garden path, and from the garden path. I had passed along the garden path.

Without having admitted the awful truth. I had not admitted the truth, that somewhere inside myself I had worried about being lost, perhaps even that I had been lost, and failed to admit it.

The place was a warren. The entire town. They called it a town. It was a large village. What was odd about human behaviour was its divergence from culture to culture, even community to community. It was species-like. Such basics as gardens, how we humans plant and design our gardens. I refer here to Christine. She would have been startled by a mention of my name in reference to gardens. I have no interest in gardens, except insofar as one may escape them. I confess it readily.

One thing she did not do was carry heavyweight bicycles for other people; nephews, grandsons, granddaughters, nieces. The purchase of said bike would not have occurred to her. Had she known this was my intention she would have taken pains to stop me, and would have succeeded (generally a shake of the head was sufficient).

Why had I bought the damn thing. He would not even want it. Youngsters have their own ideas. He would simply look at it, he would look at it.

Where was I? The gate.

Gates cannot disappear.

How strange. There it had been. But now where?

But the sense of fun does not desert us. It is the sense of fun that distinguishes the species. Who ever heard of humorous cats?

Gates do not disappear but of cats there were plenty, in this vicinity. They prowled every corner, beneath table and chair, by the town sewers, sniffing out discarded seafood, jumping onto the table tops with contaminated paws. Half the town populace had contracted kidney diseases which, in a more hysterical society, might have caused fundamental misunderstandings and proven a blight on the tourist trade. Tourist incomers congregated in particular beach restaurants and lounge bars, hoping to gain the respect of the locals. To that unlikely end they fed the local cats. But woe to them, they had misjudged the situation. They would have been as well feeding late-night snacks to a flock of capon chickens the week before xmas. The locals had a saying about cats, and dogs. It was derogatory. I cannot recollect why precisely. Nor the actual saying itself, whatever it was, to do with mouths: excess! They were excess mouths? Perhaps that was it. What else was an animal but a mouth. An excess mouth requires food. Never feed an excess mouth. No animal was worth it. Thus say the locals.

Now the gate; a mere break in the wall, but it was there, truly, an iron gate. And I recognized this from my point of entry.

Vines vines vines. Vines had concealed the gate.

Why conceal a gate? Reminiscent of the Borgias.

I moved to open the damn thing but it would not budge, it would not budge. No, it would not open. Why would it not open? It had clanged shut behind me.

I remembered this. Thus I had opened it, only an open thing can close.

What on earth was wrong with the damn thing. It would not open. The damn gate would not open, it would not open.

Gates gates. Absolute tyrants. That was the Borgias. A blemish on humanity.

The snib. I saw it. More of a bolt. A strange foreign contraption with a peculiar release-knob, circular in design. Certainly a spot of oil would have done it no harm. I grasped it with my fingers, my right hand, twisting at it. No luck. I would have to put down the bicycle. But if so having to resume the burden, for it was a burden; oh bring me to the silent shore, one might lay down one's burden, evermore evermore. The weight was proving too much. It was a ton weight on me, but at the same time, the same time

I could not release the damn snib thing with its bolt and circular damn knob thing what a peculiar design it was, completely foreign and stupidly nonfunctional, my God, in all my born days.

I did let down the bicycle, onto the damn ground, against a tree, propping it there and such relief, if shoulders had heads mine would have been light-headed and my legs rubberized stalks.

Had circumstances been more conducive I would have rested. However, I had come to distrust the owner-occupiers, given they had sold me the bicycle openly and honestly. For so it appeared. They had not shown me the exit. Thus they had not led me down the garden path. I pulled open the gate. The height of absurdity but most unfunny, I did not find it otherwise, not in the slightest. I pulled open the gate.

This matter had a serious dimension. It was not too much to ask of people that they behaved in a proper fashion to strangers, for tourists were also strangers. This pair had chosen not to show me the exit. A sad commentary on the culture.

I made to lift the bicycle. Firstly I had to free the rear wheel from a clump of weeds already taking root between the spokes; a scene from *The Day of the Triffids*, it was ludicrous.

My left shoulder had a groove from before and the bicycle frame fitted snugly. This was a literal truth. The frame fitted so snugly! I tried to insert my fingers to feel the groove along my shoulder but could not. I thought to let down the bicycle once more. I should have enjoyed a rest and should have been allowed to my God had I so desired. To sit for a moment or two. None could deny me such a thing. Least of all my grandson who would reap the benefit of the enterprise. I was not his favourite but he was mine.

No, his grandmother, he was his grandmother's boy. I did not grudge Christine this. On the contrary, it was a source of pleasure to me, that she should have experienced such love.

My granddaughters would not have wanted the bicycle, but it was not a bicycle for the girls, they were older. Nor hurt, that he was my favourite. They would have laughed. The girls still laughed at me. Likewise Christine, she used to, although we fought, often we fought.

Leadership

But for myself it was the greater challenge. The others might see it as theirs, as strangers to this practice. Not me. Never! They would begin, they would buckle down, draw strength from a trial shared. I admired and envied them for it.

My admiration was not misplaced though it surprised them. Of course they looked to me. I was the exemplar, the wonderful exemplar. For some I was glorious. Yes. And why? Because each manoeuvre lay within my grasp. So they presumed, failing to realize such mastery presents not liberation but a vast obligation; a world of obligation, overriding everything. Not only was my own life in thrall to the quest but the lives of those dearest to me.

Some chose not to see this, not to acknowledge the obligation. I cannot name them. Individuals are not functions. I accept this. At the same time they have roles, and enact them. At the same time they look to their own humanity; it is from here we begin

I regret if they are hurt by such honesty.

It is true also that I smiled. I would not deny *the* smile. This too surprised them.

Irony is to be shared. To whom did I share the smile? To whom would the smile be shared. None. I was alone. They said I was alone and were correct, an irony in itself, but unimportant if not insignificant.

If it is your life

I stopped smiling. I was on the Glasgow bus home and a woman was sitting next to me. I offered her the window seat but she preferred the aisle. Women have their own ways of doing stuff. It was that made me smile. I had a friend called Celia and she would have been exactly the same. She wanted to be an actress, or actor as she said. She memorized lines from classic plays; angry ones with big statements. She spoke them aloud or acted the parts. Even walking down the street. It was quite embarrassing. A pal of mine from boyhood did the same. Even with him I found it embarrassing. With Celia I pretended not to bother. But she saw that it did. If she had known the true extent she would have scorned me. No wonder. It was a hopeless brand of self-consciousness, worse than the ordinary. And arrogant too. It did not seem to be but it was. What right did I have to be self-conscious of something she was doing? That was so arrogant.

I had not thought of it in that way and it was true. Males are arrogant. I did not see myself as arrogant at all, not in the slightest, so it was like a compliment.

Even thinking about her, it was nice, she was just so jees, sexy, really, even on the bus and thinking about her, enjoying it in my own head. It was nice. But sad too, but life can be sad. Usually on long bus trips I just read or stared out the window.

Celia was so acute in her observations, very much so. People had to respect that. Especially in a woman. Women are different. There is no question about that. I had a sister, a mother and grandmother and that meant nothing. I did not know women, I did not know them at all. Celia studied people and I could see how this must be essential for anyone who wanted to become an actor. I thought she would be great at it. I respected her more than anyone, more than myself. Much more. I learned from her, even being in her presence. Not only did I appreciate her own lack of self-consciousness I began noticing it in others. Those that had it seemed satisfied with themselves. Not in a bad way. I did not see them as 'smug'. They were content with themselves, or *within* themselves. Maybe it was an illusion. I saw them out and about and their lips were moving. They were not phoning, not texting. Some had earphones and actively engaged with the music, whether singing along or performing actions with their limbs. Others sang on their own account. They were not listening to anything except out their own head. Or in their own head, inside it. From inside it. Inside within it. You listened to things inside your own head, from inside.

Or did you? Did people listen inside or from inside?

Ears are outside but your hearing is inside. If we look at our heads in a practical manner we gain insights. It seems obvious and it is obvious. But so obvious people never do it.

If you were singing you were not listening. Maybe singing into yourself. Not out loud. A lot of people did that. They walked along the road singing away to themselves. Eric Semple was the worst, an old pal of mine. He sang out loud. It was like he was on stage. You would not have minded if it was walking along the street but he did it at other times too, like on the bus. People could hear him. Talk about embarrassing. That really was. I thought so anyway. He did not. Him and Celia were the same there. It was only me. I was the one that worried.

Why? Why worry about other people. It was not a pleasant trait and I wished I did not have it. People should be allowed to get on with their own lives without others butting in. Ones like me.

I thought too much about other people. I could not stop myself and did not feel good doing it. I saw Eric at the Christmas break and it was a fight. I got annoyed with him because he got annoyed with me. He said I was giving him a telling-off. It was not a telling-off. It was just that stupid singing. Maybe he did not know he was doing it. But other people were there and could hear. Why did he not sing into himself? I could not understand that. But deep down I knew why, he was getting at me. It was because I had left home to go to university. It was a mixture of jealousy and I do not know what, except things had changed. But it was not me changing them. There was no point blaming me.

He was annoyed and I did not know why. I thought he was going to walk away. We were in one of the few under-21 bars in town. He liked his beer so for him to walk away was a big thing. Although he looked older than me and probably would have got served in other places. He was fuming. It made me smile seeing him. That only made it worse, swearing at me. What the fuck are you laughing at?

I was not laughing I was only smiling. I was glad to be having a pint with him. You are just annoying me, he said.

I dont mean to.

That made it worse. Eric drank his beer down. He was a bigger drinker than me when it came to pints. I preferred bottles. Pints were too much, if you took too many; and Eric did, although he could handle it. I used to be able to. I was out the habit. People did not drink so much down south. One beer lasted for ages. Some drank wine, glasses of wine. If you were in company together you might order a bottle and you all shared it. It was just different. If me and Eric went out while I was home it would be to a pub and it would be beer. It would be nice seeing him this time but not if it was another fight. I made him angry. But he made me angry. He blamed me for stuff that was not my fault – talking posh. How come you're talking posh? I was not talking posh. I was saying things properly, or trying to. There is a difference. If I did not say things properly people did not know what I was talking about. It was bad enough as it was. I was not being a snob, I was just sick of people not understanding me, or pretending they did not. Sometimes I thought they pretended.

Celia understood when I explained it. She even noticed it. But Eric got more annoyed and then went off into his 'so' routine. Every time I explained something it was 'So?'

So? So? So?

So I felt like punching him on the mouth, that was so. Surely he had passed the 'so' stage. He had being doing it since he was five years of age. We all did but some grew out it. He did not, at least not with me. You could say 'so' to everything. That was what he did. It was stupid: stupid *and* meaningless. Not completely. But how come he did not understand the point I was making whereas somebody who was English under-stood completely. And not Celia, I was not referring to her. He thought I was but I was not. I did not want to talk about her, and not about sex. He did not want me talking about her either. Although he acted like he did anyway, that was what I thought. So what, I was not going to, who cares.

Anyway, it was Rob Anderson I was talking about, the best lecturer at university. Because of his attitude to the students. He called it the 'so question'. Rob had two children of his own and this is what they did, 'So?' He thought it insightful; without the 'so question' there would have been no Socrates. It kept you on your toes, speaking intellectually. Much of Rob's own philosophy came from observing children. So he said anyway although children did not read Plato, which is what Celia said. Typical Celia. But she was right in a way. Celia did not do philosophy but she came out and said things that were strong, even when it was to do with Rob Anderson, it did not worry her.

The woman beside me was reading a thick paperback book, her wee light beaming down. It was a costume-drama, I saw the cover. Damsels in distress and knights in shining armour! The wee light made it more atmospheric, just that peace and quiet.

People read what they wanted. I read private-eye stories, different ones, not just Chandler, people said Chandler but I liked other ones. Rob read detective stories too. I was surprised at that but he was not and I should not have been. The philosopher Wittgenstein was a favourite of his and if I did a third-year course then I would meet with him. He was difficult. People said that. He sounded interesting because of that. But he read detective stories, Wittgenstein. A lot of philosophers did.

People were ordinary, philosophers or not. You did not read heavy stuff all the time. Not even if you were heavy. Philosophers were 'heavy' but that did not mean they only read 'heavy' books. It was the same if you were studying, you had to switch off occasionally.

Even looking out the window and the peace and quiet, that was the M6 the farther north you went. And with night-time. I loved it. People were tired and away in their own thoughts, just thinking about whatever it was – going home, that was me.

You were just very aware it was England. That was what I thought. It was so different. I liked it. I did not say that to my parents or anybody but it was true. Who wanted to be in Glasgow all the time! And for the rest of your life! No thanks. The world was big, just so so big. Celia's brother lived in New York, or New York City, that was what she called it.

She was so absolutely different to anything. There were no other girls like her. The idea of meeting one like her in Glasgow. Unless maybe you were up the West End round the Byres Road area or else Sauchiehall Street; some place with students, otherwise where? Nowhere.

My head went everywhere, and seeing the moon too, just everything. The thing about her, how sexy she was. You were not supposed to talk about that. Ha ha. Well it did not apply to her! Because she would have been the first, and I was the one if anybody did, knowing about it, because I did. It made you smile. Because people would never think, seeing me, they would never ever think, and yet, that was them, it was up to them.

The woman beside me too, imagine her; she would never ever think. Nobody would. I had not been naked before. I had had sex a lot of times, quite a few; of course I had but not like with Celia, just naked the two of us and her not caring, just with her breasts, just flopping, not caring. People would not know that, seeing me, never, and her pubic hair, just to see. They never ever would think it. And at university too, never. I would never tell them a thing anyway, never ever.

Sex is sex. But not for women. There were no pals anyway that I would have told. But I would tell Eric. I would. I think I would. I wanted to. Sometimes when you wanted to say something you did not get the chance. People spoke about their own stuff.

She did not want me to say anything. She did not say it but I knew. But I was not going to tell anybody.

But it made me smile. Because of the dark outside and the wee light beaming down my face was clear in its reflection and I had a smile, and it was a strange smile. Not like my smile. It was a different type of smile. I did not like it, although in some ways I did. It was Mister Hyde smiling back at Doctor Jekyll. There is an evil glint in his eye but a horrible irony as well and it is lurking there and like another story I read in Edgar Allan Poe which was just brilliant; warped sides of the one individual. Some writers were brilliant. They were like philosophers and just stayed in your mind.

Every event has a cause. For every one thing a thing happens in succession. Except the world, if you regard the world as an event but maybe not. The world is not really an event, just a thing in itself. Unless if it is God, if you believe in God then you might argue the point, God caused the world. Or if God is the cause. So the world is His effect. Take away God and that is the world, what happens to it? Gone.

These are things you would say. I loved the subject, if you would call it a subject. The great thing about philosophy is that it is actual life, it is hardly a subject at all. Some treated it as a subject and that was their downfall; they might score good marks in class but true understanding would not come from that form of study. Okay they might get good results but beyond that no.

Eric would have been good at philosophy. Harder for Celia. She went her own way and at a certain point there has to be *the* way, if only as a beginning. Once you begin go where you want but let us begin from that same point, if you can find it. That is the trouble, but if you do find it then it becomes the whole world. Or the whole world becomes, it is just there and all alive. It is marvellous. That was Descartes, what a hero! He was the one we were given and you just felt lucky, imagine it was Hobbes or Locke, you would just shudder.

I could not imagine Celia and Eric ever meeting. They were both aliens. She would not fit into his world and neither would he in hers. Yet they were both mine. His world was my world before leaving Glasgow. A woman like Celia could not exist in Glasgow. Perhaps she could but I could not imagine it. Or a guy like Eric Semple at university down south. I could never imagine that either. People would not understand him. It was a separate brand of humour. You saw things differently; your whole way of thinking. Almost like it was disconnected. Eric could have gone to a Scottish university, although maybe not Edinburgh, and never St Andrews. Never an English one.

It was class. I did not show my class but Eric did. This is what it was. My dad spoke about it; to him it was everything. It explained everything. He believed in Karl Marx. Rob Anderson did not disagree with my father on that. In his opinion the academics underrated Marx as a 'thinker'. They said he was not 'first rate'. Some were 'first rate'. In philosophy only the 'first rate' mattered. But even there, you would not find him on any syllabus. Rob thought it disgraceful. He found it *salient* the way they ignored Marx and others from a different culture or background. Even Jean-Paul Sartre and the Germans. The academics stayed with their own people and kept others out.

But what was striking about the Glasgow bus home, right at that minute in time, and you noticed it immediately, and you could not help but notice, that everybody, every last person on the entire bus, each single solitary one was Scottish, they all had accents and were ordinary accents; none was posh. The woman next to me as well, she did not smile or even look at me but I knew. I did not find it relaxing; I do not think I did. I was the same as them but on the other hand was I? Maybe I was not. And what if there were others in a similar situation? It was like we were each one of us disconnected, each one of us, until we were on the bus home, and starting to become Scottish again, Scottish working class. My father would have said that, never to forget it, because they would never allow it.

It was a peculiar thing altogether. Once Rob Anderson came to the pub with some of us and we had a few beers. He was saying stuff and making people laugh. He said to me when no one else was listening that I should be careful, there were those who would not wish me well. He came from a town in Yorkshire and said it happened to him. He was resigned to it. He could reach a stage but not progress further, because of his background. He said he had a Yorkshire accent. You would hear it if you listened. But he was proud of Yorkshire, very much so, and enjoyed sports, especially cricket and rugby. Those were the two most popular, by far. It was hard to find even one football fan. I asked Rob which team he supported but he only said he had a soft spot for them all if they were Yorkshire, Yorkshire teams. But what if it was Sheffield United and Sheffield Wednesday? He just smiled when I said that. So I knew he did not really bother; you cannot have two sides if they are rivals; either one or none but not two.

I missed playing football. There were teams at uni, including five-a-sides, but I did not know guys who played. I could find out and was going to.

But what Rob said about the other academics was interesting. Celia did not know him but thought he must have been bitter to think that way. She was dubious. Under his influence I would be ripe for paranoia. That is what she said. But I watched other academics; they rarely spoke to students, even to say hullo. It happened to me at the end of second term, in the same lift as my sociology tutor and he did not look at me. Yet he knew fine well that I was in his tutorial group. I did not care. But it was weird. My father said nothing but he agreed with me, I know he did. Mum did not. She did not believe they were intentionally rude. Mum thought the best of people. Dad hated hearing about them. Be the best at your lessons son, then they cannot ignore you. That was what he said, then went back to his newspaper.

Maybe it was true. But I was not the best at my lessons. I soon found that out. I did not tell mum and dad.

I did not tell them everything; especially dad, it was easier with mum. But when I told her things they would reach him sooner or later. The same if I told my young sister, she would tell mum and mum would tell dad. Family politics, that was how it worked in mine.

I was looking forward to going home. I had been back at Christmas but only a few days. I returned to England the day before New Year and it caused bother. Mum got upset because of it and did not come out her bedroom when I was leaving. But there was no bus on New Year's day so it was either wait or go the day before. It was not as if I did not enjoy being there, of course I did, and seeing everybody, it was great.

My life had changed so much. Probably it would be harder to communicate now than it had been at Christmas, and Christmas had not been easy. But that was life. And my own fault for not coming home before that. Mum was right to be hurt. She was hurt. Dad was hurt too but acted as if he was not. My sister told me. But what was I supposed to do? It was difficult. I would have failed all my essays if I had not worked through the holiday period. I was not brilliant. They thought I was but I knew I was not. Some were. I was not. In school I was but not down there.

Oh but not even in school, I was not brilliant, I could just answer everything and do it all but that was our school, an ordinary school, not like theirs down south; their parents paid a fortune, more than my father earned in a year. That is true. It was him told me but it was correct what he said. I was in the low half down there whereas up home I was top or else near the top. They were completely different down south. Most of them were clever but the brilliant ones really were brilliant. That was their good luck.

I liked being there when they were all away, especially in the library and finding places tucked away, wee study corners. I flew through my essays, it was great. I did not know Celia at that time. Imagine I did and she had not gone home! if it had just been the two of us, if she had stayed at uni, jeesoh, ye think of that, except the essays, that was the silly thing, I would have missed the deadlines or else done hopeless. Just seeing her all the time, if I could. But she would not anyway. I only saw her when she wanted; sometimes not for a week. More than a week. We had not had sex for eighteen days. One week she had not been there so that does not count but the other days she was. Unless it was her period. I did not think it was. Eighteen days. I did not see her all the time. But she liked sex.

I never had sex before, not properly where you were in bed all night and you could just even go to sleep and wake up and then just well more sex, you could, it was just so so different from anything, Celia was just so different. No point talking. No point, just it was all so different.

My life had changed so much. It was true. Jeesoh. Out the window, seeing the night sky. Rugged in Scotland, over the border. The woman next to me was still reading. I wished I could read like that. Damsels in distress, I did not realize sex would be like that. I knew it was great but I did not think, just how with Celia and in my arms and all night too; you just shivered. Her skin was even different. I could touch her.

It was so true.

And my young sister too, how with her secrets; girls had secrets, and about their body, it was all secrets; how else could you say it.

Things had really changed. It could never be the same. And with my sister. Just strange, strange thinking about it, my little sister, but she was a woman and if she had a boyfriend. It was the way of the world, if you touched her, or she touched you; a woman, it was so so different. If you were dancing and how you looked, you would be looking but the woman would not look at you, because if she did; if you looked at each other and then smiled, if she smiled at you, it was just shivering, you shivered, you just got hard, it was all just sex, it was just so amazing and I had not known it before. I knew it but I did not.

I was looking forward to seeing Eric and going for a beer. He had been a good pal. He was a funny guy. He kept you going with his stupid patter. Although how could it be called stupid. It was not. If it was intentional, and it was, then it was not stupid. How could it be? He would have made a great stand-up comedian. I had not seen him for a while. I had not seen anybody for a while but I had not been home since last September, excluding Christmas; Christmas did not count. I was only there a couple of days and hardly saw a soul. He was the only one apart from family.

I would need to get out. I could not stay in the house all the time.

Probably he still sang in public. Unless he had hit the big time! Now I smiled. Although you never know. Somebody had to!

But maybe he used that as an excuse. Maybe that was why he did it, he was preparing for the day he won a major talent show!

Did he honestly believe that! Maybe he did. The stupid side was obvious. But he was not a mug, he would have seen that too, as much as anyone. But there was another side to that: Eric himself. Somebody had to win. He had as much chance as anybody. Probably more because he believed in himself. He did, really! He thought people wanted to hear him sing! Me too, he actually thought I wanted to hear him!

It was a personal quirk. Even if you told him to shut up he did not believe you, he thought you were saying it for effect. Secretly you wanted to hear him. He honestly believed that. Even when we were boys! What an ego! I had forgotten about that. His self-belief was much stronger than mine. In comparison I had an inferiority complex.

But at what point is self-belief transformed into egocentricity? If we were walking up the road, just the two of us, and he started singing I found it embarrassing. He must have thought I was a total fool. It irritated me. Eventually I told him, Oh fuck off man. I done that a few times but he still did it. So it was not to annoy me. It had nothing to do with me. He even did it when he was on his own. I watched him and I saw him perform wee actions, wee actions, and he was only there himself. It was a characteristic he shared with Celia. But at that time me and him were still at school and it was just weird. I kind of worried about him, doing something like that in public, it was beyond embarrassing.

Seriously. Eric was my best pal but it made you wonder about him. Yet some of what he did was the same as Celia. So if it was okay for her why not for him? Was that another gender issue? If so it put a different complexion on matters. It was illogical anyway. Unless it was separate logical systems. Some said that about women, that they operate differently from males in a structural sense. A guy said that in our sociology tutorial. He was destroyed. People ridiculed him. One of the girls wanted to punch him which only made him worse. He sounds likeable but he was not. He was arrogant, completely unlikeable, and not good-looking at all, but chubby, and with a chubby face. His dad was something like a Member of Parliament or town mayor. I told my mother about him. She would tell my father. I could not have told him. There were things I could not tell him and that was one. He liked me being at university in England but there were certain things he could not listen to me talking about. Usually to do with class. The idea of somebody in my tutorial group with a famous father or if he was rich. My father could not listen. I stopped talking about stuff if he was there, I mean political stuff.

Eric was like my father. I wanted to tell him stuff but he got annoyed and it was me he got annoyed with.

I came out sounding bad but it was not me so much as a class thing, male working class. I did not need Celia to tell me.

I was not stepping on anybody's shoulders. It is a cliché about people escaping from their background, how they step on the shoulders of friends and family. Eric could have gone to university himself. He was bright. Definitely. Why had he not? Perhaps his family did not push him. But they would have. I knew his parents. They were better off than mine but also they would have appreciated the chance. So why had he not gone? It was a chance in life none of our parents ever had. No matter how I might feel on a personal level I made the best of it. It would have been self-indulgent not to, and selfish.

Selfishness was all around. I saw it at university. Self-indulgence too.

But you needed money for stuff and I never had it, not really, and the bar job I had was for essentials. It was killing my parents for fees so the least I could do was be careful. Too much of anything. Stuff did not interest me anyway. And other people's company was the same. You had to push your way in. I could not be bothered. Probably they thought I was boring. Maybe I was. Celia said I was relaxing. Probably that meant boring. They all had money. I thought they did anyway. You needed money. Most seemed to have it. But maybe they did not. People pretended and were scared to be different. I already was because I was Scottish. Some liked me because of it, others did not. It would be wrong to say

I did not care. I was just glad to know Celia. And her father was in business. I did not care. Her mother even, she was a doctor. Doctors are rich.

I liked her attitude to everything, and how she was, how she thought, it was always herself and not other people's prejudices. If it was left-wing politics or right-wing, she would want to know about the person, what like was the person. That to me was important. In Glasgow it was where you came from. People were scared to be different. My mother was like that. My father was a bit; if it was somebody that was upper class or else the royal family, he hated all that and would not listen to it or read it and if it was on the television he would switch channels or get up and leave the room, it did not matter the person. When I told Celia about him she listened and then said a funny thing, Does he whistle? My dad did, sometimes Mozart and Beethoven. Imagine classical! We were talking about old people. Her father was an old man compared to mine. Really, he was like a grandfather and over sixty years of age. Mine was forty-four and my mother forty-three. Celia was surprised. She was saying how old people talked to themselves and it was a good thing. But it was only men who sang. Men did not suffer from a foolish self-consciousness. Women did. They had to break through a barrier. Even Celia. She memorized her lines and said them aloud but she did not sing. Women did not, not in public. And they did not whistle. Men whistled. They did it on buses the way Eric sang. It was nearly as embarrassing, especially if women were there because you were a male as

well and it was childish behaviour. We did not all behave
the same way. Men were men but we were not all the
same.

Women did not whistle. Had I ever heard one woman
whistle? Never. It was a distinguishing feature. A very
striking one. Here was a wee minor detail yet it separated the sexes, every bit as much as the sexual organs.
Obviously not to that extent but it was a distinguishing
feature. Yet I could not remember having read about it
before.

Women always watched themselves. Men did not,
except in a showing-off way. But women showed off
too, especially about sex and their bodies. I had sex with
two women here; once the first time and then Celia.
Celia was just so different. She was an only child. That
could mean something. It could explain her lack of self-
consciousness. No need for privacy. With wee sisters
you watch so she does not see you dressing or catch
you peeing in the bathroom. This means you are always
aware of your surroundings, and aware of yourself
within them, within your surroundings. You see yourself. You need to. But Celia would have done what she
liked and just, she could just have undressed without
worrying because nobody would have been there to
see her, just wandering around, she could have, if she
wanted. That was what she did. She took me to her
room and other women lived there and she wandered
around only in her pants and even no bra sometimes
and the women knew I was there, they knew I was in
her room, so I was seeing her. Celia did not bother and

then if she came back to bed and we started doing
things and it was not quiet. So I admired her too, as a
human being. She behaved in a proper way. Human
beings should be allowed that, to be the same. It is dignity. People have it. Women have it, and Celia with big
breasts flopping, because they did, and heavy, if you put
your hands under and held them and just if you held
them. But it was dignity, it was a woman, although you
could never have been a runner, unless they were
strapped down. But women were runners, they were
athletes, so they must have been. It was just dignity, it
was just being a woman. That is what Celia was. She
thought about herself and what she was involved in,
she became engrossed in it and absorbed.

So too if she was saying lines. It was the same with
other people, they did not all want to be actors. Maybe
they did. I doubt it. Probably they enjoyed quoting from
plays, books and movies; that was that and nothing
more. It could even be dialogue. Imagine doing dialogue out loud, saying different voices, asking questions
and answering them, walking along the road by yourself! Some folk must have. If you saw them you would
think they were having a real conversation, except it
was with themself like in a movie with a psychological
plot, maybe if it was a schizophrenic subject, say a guy
had different personalities. Or it could be a woman;
people trying to control her, and all inside her head all
different personalities with all different names. It was
quite scary. These personalities did not have to be fighting
for supremacy. It could just be an ordinary conversation

they were having. Just an ordinary one. And it could be any topic. Except the person whose head it was, the woman with the schizophrenic problem, she could not be the topic, not her herself; that was the one thing the different personalities never discussed, the only taboo topic. Imagine they all discussed the actual person whose head they were in! As soon as they done that the problem became acute, and what next? Madness? It would be a great story to read. That would be like Edgar Allan Poe or else Robert Louis Stevenson. Madness would be next. Although not necessarily, it just depended on the extent of the problem. Even if it was a problem. Maybe it was not or they had yet to discover it was a problem. That condition happens to people and they fail to realize it is happening. Until it does, right out the blue, some traumatic event; a murder usually, the person kills somebody, or one personality tries to kill another. That would be like suicide. But it would not be suicide. That is the amazing thing. It would be the opposite, so what is that, murder, although people would say suicide; they would think it was because it was the one human being. Theoretically no, it would be murder. And they would have to use poison because it would seem like it was happening to somebody else whereas if they used a knife the personalities would know immediately. Jesus Christ I am stabbing myself! Why am I doing it! Why is this happening! You would be murdering yourself except you would not be. You could imagine an actor doing it, a good actor, and all the facial changes.

I was not keen on drama before. We got it at school. To me it was the worst kind of arrogance. Ego, ego. I changed my mind because with Celia. She loved the actual plays. This is why she wanted to do it, not like the other ones. They also acted but it was just stupid; the whole thing was stupid, and nothing to do with great plays and literature. People kidded on it was. It was not serious, just amateur rubbish like you got on television. Celia was in two theatre companies; one at uni and one in the town where her parents lived. The students' one was Shakespeare and the town one was murders or comedies – they were called comedies. I read a couple and they were diabolical stupidity.

She asked me to do it. The students' company wanted fresh faces, especially men and if you were macho. I was not macho but it was nice she said it, quite like a compliment. I knew it was the Scottish accent, 'rough and ready'. She wanted me to go to a practice 'read-through'. This was one by Henrik Ibsen, the Norwegian author. His plays had great parts for women, *Hedda Gabler*. I quite wanted to because with her there and just being part of it. The company did practice 'read-throughs' by other authors apart from Shakespeare; Arthur Miller was one. Sometimes people did not turn up, especially at exam time. If I came it would be helpful. I nearly did go but then no. I could appreciate the play and it was a laugh doing it. I did the English accent and got it quite good. But why did it have to be the English accent if it was Norwegian, why not Scottish? 'I am sorry Mrs Hedda, but I fear I must dispel an amiable illusion.'

People would smile when I said it. But why? If it is Norwegian it is Norwegian, so it should be any language.

Because I was the only Scottish person.

That was not much of an argument.

Celia did not care. It was only a read-through anyway.

But what did that mean? If it was an actual play and people were doing proper acting, would it have to be English?

The habit she had was beautiful. She put her hand on the side of my face and stared into my eyes as if looking inside me. She only cared that I said the lines when we were outside and walking down the street.

But I could not, even for fun. 'I fear I must dispel an amiable illusion.' I could say the lines in her room quite easily but not outside. I had to not see people's faces. Oh but surely I could mouth it.

No, I could not. I would have got a red face. I got red faces everywhere. I always got them, just blushing all the time. In tutorials or wherever, it was terrible.

And of course I wanted to be involved because it was obvious because how one thing was how it led to sex, if it was inside or outside. I noticed how she ended up and it was wanting me, wanting sex with me. Ohh. She pinched my arm. We were going along the road and she finished her lines and she did it, maybe just saying Ohh, and then pinching me on the upper arm and turning half on to me as we walked. It made me hard, and walking along the street, I told her, how I was to walk, she laughed. That was a thing how she laughed. She did not laugh at much but me and sex, I made her laugh. She liked me because I got hard. Just thinking about her, jeesoh. Wherever, I could not sit down, or stand up, having to disguise it all the time. She laughed at that and walking along the street and her hand in my pocket, she did that just to get me and she always did, always, she did not care, just her hand.

I got jealous. That was a problem. She did not like jealous people. I did not think I was jealous and when she said I was I thought it a wee bit of a compliment but it was not a compliment. It meant I was naive and ridiculous. Because there had to be other people in her life, the world was full of people and that was freedom, she needed freedom.

It might sound daft but maybe doing philosophy worked against me. I was aware of myself too much and what I thought: what did it matter what I thought; but it did, and in the world too, how my thought mattered in the world; how it mattered to other human beings, and the one source of truth and the absolute base, that was all humanity, and I was part of it and of course Celia herself, what we two thought as separate human beings. She was so honest but if she said something and it was not what I thought I had to say it or else just not talk, better not to talk, so it was better I did not talk.

She never got angry, it was me. But her face went red and she stared right into me seeing what it was, what did I want, it was up to me.

It *was* up to me. That was right enough. Even if she wanted me to do something, and I knew she did: I did not have to do it.

It was me stopped it. I had not seen her for a while but it was me, my fault. She was with somebody else. I knew she would be. Some rich guy, way out of my league; Oxford or Cambridge or whatever. He would be rich, talking about mummy and daddy all the time; diddums and middums. One did speak like that. Unless she was joking. That was her, diddums and middums. Big mummies' boys. That was what she said. She might not have been telling the truth. Are you jealous? Why are you jealous? There is nothing to be jealous about.

You could only be jealous if you were the same as somebody else. She said people were all unique and individuals so how could you be jealous, it was nonsensical.

Sometimes she was like a snob. Other times she was the most unsnobbish person you could meet. If she liked people it did not matter lower class or upper class, only if they had a certain view of the world to do with being free and relaxed or all wound up and roped into society's social spheres. You had to rise above society. The people she admired were above it. It did not matter their background, even royalty. Individuals were unique and could do anything, and not be hidebound. Class did not enter into it, lower or higher.

What did that mean, lower or higher?

I almost laughed when she told me that. It was my father. I should have laughed. I was too respectful. I should have been more – something, different anyway, different to myself. If I wanted to be. But I did not want to be. I would have said the same as her if it was to my dad. But hearing Celia say it made me into him. Okay Celia was interested in people. But only if they were interesting, that is what I thought. Or if she liked them, it was because they were likeable. But who were they likeable for? Her. Who were they being interesting for? Her.

Some of them were pure bastards. I thought that. I did not know them but knew I would hate them.

It is working-class. Not lower-class. Not lower-class, *working*-class. I told her that and swore.

Why was I so angry?

I was angry just because, just because, that was why I was so angry, yes and so so angry. She did not mind me swearing. If I said 'fuck' and apologized she was like why apologize. Do not apologize, not if it is the way you talk.

I talk however I talk, it is up to me.

Yes, she said. And the way she said it, really, it was patronizing. I knew that. So did she. Her face flushed red. She knew she done it. She saw *my* face. She knew I knew. She did. She would never have cried in her whole life. Never, just looking at me so I wanted to hold her, of course I did. I wanted to hold her and just hold her and if I did it was too tight and she disliked it and disliked me doing it and I had to stop and control myself. I held her too tightly, it was too tightly, far too tightly, and hurt her. Only because I wanted her so much, that was the trouble. I had to calm down. She told me that too. That was the trouble, she was my one and only friend. I could have had more but I did not want them. Maybe I would in future, if I went back. I had not decided to go back. That was the wee germ inside me. Now that I thought it I knew it was there. I had a stack of books and two essay workings in my backpack; maybe I would take them out and dump them. Out the window. Except a bus. Who cares.

Celia said it to me about calming down. Not to do with her but in general, I became too angry and emotional. But I felt angry and anger is emotional. There was only one academic I could talk to in the entire place and that was Rob Anderson. Every other one was an elitist shit. The whole place was elitist. He was even elitist. He was talking to me and I did not know why he was talking to me; asking about football why was he asking about football what did it matter about football, he did not care about it. It was for me, for my benefit. There were these Scottish working-class things and people said them to me. Which one do you support, meaning Rangers or Celtic. I hate the two of them. They just looked at you, they did not know what you were talking about. Somebody like me, you had to be one or the other, just stereotypes all the time.

It was incredible how elitist it was. People did not know how bad it was. Most students were elitist. Black as well as white, and Asians, foreigners, everybody. I found it shocking. The entire bunch. Celia was the only one I could relate to. Not because she was a woman. What did it matter, women or men, it was just how they treated you. I did not have an idealized view of women. She said I did. I did not think so. It was competition, I was not in competition. Anyway, not with her.

But for her. I could not compete for her. I did not want to.

I did not know about this world. I had my place in it. It did not matter what I did. It would have been great to go away someplace, take a year out, if I could work a bar somewhere like in Australia or New Zealand. If I just finished the year, I had to finish the year which meant going back after the break. Probably I would, just study hard and finish the essays. Who cares. My reflection in the window reminded me of a movie. None in particular.

Here was a young guy travelling on a bus, from one large city to another, a longer than usual trip and the bus did not have a toilet. The driver drove into services along the motorway, and also dropped off passengers, picked other ones up. The last stop in England was always good. People got off, the ones that smoked smoked. It was always freezing cold. It was! That was funny. I was always freezing, and shivering, glad to get back in the bus.

What if I did not! Departing forever. He departed the bus. The young man departed the bus. What if I just got off again, and did not come back?

There was nowhere to go. No money to spare. I had a part-time job and needed every penny to help my parents. University was dear.

I preferred long journeys. I did not want to get to places. What if your journey lasted forever? The young man was seeing his face in the window and smiling but then it was not, it was evil and terrified and horrible, a face in the dark shadows of the window.

It would be a French movie, not American. But it could be American, depending on the director. But French was the more likely, or East European, or Southeast Asian. That fitted more, if it was under the yoke of a foreign power. I wished I knew more about politics. I was going to take a class but then did not. People thought they knew about politics but they did not, only about parliament. If I was with Celia and her friends they were cautious because of me. But I did not care. They could say what they liked. Anyway, I did not know about the Scottish Nationalists. My parents were socialists. My dad especially but mum too. They knew about politics. Older people did.

But other stuff was important. How one thought about things was important. That was my opinion. My dad spoke about working-class struggles and it was not like from a book, or students talking in the union bar but even with him, if he had known some philosophy, I think it would have helped him.

Why did people not know philosophy? If they did it would be good.

Old people saw politics in action. My last time on this bus was returning to uni after the Christmas break. An old man sat beside me and that was what he talked about; battles with the police, getting battered by them. My dad talked about it too. But this old man was way older than dad, he was elderly; going to stay with his daughter in Kent. You could not get farther south. He smiled when he said it. He meant it was farthest away from Scotland. If he had had his time over that is what he would have done, got as far away from Scotland as he could. He said that to me. I just smiled but he meant it. He was interested in me talking. What did I have to say? But I did not have anything to say. Except personal stuff and I did not want to say about that. It was not anybody's business, him or anybody else. I had had a fight with Eric Semple before getting on the bus. He came to say cheerio then he said about Hogmanay too, the same as my mother, imagine not staying for Hogmanay. My goodness that was all I needed was him. Really, I was sick of it, and mum staying in the bedroom, that was the last thing I needed was Eric. Even my dad, he was just looking at me: what like it was my fault it was not my fault. That was unfair.

Elderly people want these conversations with you. I found that with them, as if they are close friends. It is a nice characteristic. They take things for granted and do not care about minor details. Like bodies, knees. His knee kept banging into mine and even lying against it. How did you react to that? I did not know except just relax, what did it matter, even if the person was gay, you just had to not worry about stuff. He did not care, probably did not even notice. Maybe old people lose a sense of touch. Imagine I had banged my knee into the woman in the seat beside me? She would have slapped my face. Maybe not. Your bodies have to touch when you sit together. Bodies are bodies but do not make a *fetish* of them. That was Celia; *fetish*. She had relationships with women too and these were ambiguous, they really were. One time in the union bar she was lying with her head in another woman's lap. She was. What did that mean? Not sex surely. But if ambiguous was the word then surely that is what it meant. If a thing is ambiguous there is a sexual connotation. What other word could it be? The elderly man's knee was not ambiguous, not for one minute, he was just a good old guy. I thought he was, he did not care about bodies.

These relationships Celia had could not be sexual. She had the same with men, intense relationships. She had them with everybody. Why could she not say hullo to people! Surely that was enough? You do not have to have conversations with them all, asking after everybody's parents and brothers and sisters, who cares about all that, not for everybody, everybody in the whole world it is just impossible, so why even try, it just kills you.

That was old people. Why were they always so interested? It could be irritating.

I felt that about Celia, without being critical. I got angry at myself too. She said these things, stupid things, and I should not have taken them seriously. It was my fault. Everybody is working class. She said it to me. We all have to work.

Imagine my dad hearing that. Just silly stuff. She must have thought that about me, that I was silly.

Maybe I was. I asked her and she did that thing, looking into my eyes. For the 'real me'. Maybe that is what she was looking for. It was just silly. What is a human being?

Okay she did not have to like me but she slept with me. Why? Was it because I was Scottish? Scottish working class?

Did she like me?

There was a way of looking at Scotland from English people. I caught it from Rob Anderson. He was cautious when he said things; he watched to see my response. That was funny. What did he think!

I did not know. Not Celia either. I know she did not 'love' me. That big word. I know she did not.

Because.

I knew it.

I asked her about liking me and she could not say it. She was honest. She would never lie.

Maybe we were finished forever. It was my fault. I would have been better not speaking. I did not speak. Sometimes I did. Sometimes I did anything, whatever I wanted, and if I did not go back, maybe I would never go back. Really, in a way I did not want to.

The rain pouring down. It was noisy. Beating off the window. Smacking off the window. I looked like a wee person, my reflection, a wee worried face. I smiled to see it, and was glad. Then the woman beside me shifted on her seat to see out. That is heavy, she said, my God. You always know when you cross the border. It is always raining.

I smiled. I maybe said 'yes'.

It was interesting too how women's secrets, you know all your life about women but really you know nothing. This woman did not know about me and would think I knew nothing but it was not true.

I could even think things! Seeing her, I could! I did not. But I could have, even her age, she was like what age – I do not know. Near to mum.

That was Eric, he was just any woman, that was a joke, he was just like any woman at all and talking about it all the time, usually he was, sex, just all the time. Except now Celia. Maybe he was jealous. I thought he was. Things had changed. I had changed.

The woman closed the book and settled back in her seat, probably closing her eyes. I did not look to see in case she was awake. She had been reading for hours! If you could read text books for hours you would be a genius. Sometimes if it was philosophy it took hours for one sentence; everytime I opened the book I had to go back to the same place.

One thing though, I was starving. I had not thought about food until now. There is something in our sub-conscious world. Something said by the woman sparked it off, or was it myself, how I responded to her? Something in me. It was hours since I ate. I wondered if she had brought food with her, maybe sand-wiches; people brought sandwiches for long bus journeys. Usually I forgot and just bought a bar of chocolate. Perhaps if she had sandwiches she would offer me one!

Why did I even think of that? Because she was a woman. It was sexist. The woman takes care of the food.

But women do. Not all women. Celia did fancy stuff sometimes, not often, hardly at all. She went for hours without eating; if I had waited for her I would have starved to death. Anything I made she ate; cheese on toast, anything, scrambled eggs and beans, pilchards or sardines, fried onions and veggie sausages, rolls and potato crisps: anything at all, I had to do it because she would not, a sausage sandwich even. So much so you wondered if she was actually lazy. Why did she not cook? Yet she ate anything! She gave you the idea she was fussy but she was not. She had a big appetite but pretended not to have. She did not have to pretend. I did not care. Even I liked her appetite. Only I did not notice it at first. If I bought food when we were out she just laughed but she ate it and if it was fish and chips walking home from the movies, she loved it. Just the whole thing. But I loved it more because it was sexy. I thought it was. Sex and food. People say that and you get movies about it; I saw a great Japanese one with Celia. Another one too and it was erotic, I did not think it would be, I did not think of Japanese people having erotic movies. I thought it was the 'degenerate West'. I was not a movie buff but she was. But it was good being with her there and usually it was quiet when we went. She liked me stroking her. One time after it we returned to her place and people were there and all talking together. They all seemed to know each other except me but it was like they knew who I was. But they did not talk to me and I thought they excluded me. And Celia said something and it was like she excluded me too. Maybe I misheard. I do not even know what it was and have forgotten about it almost completely, it was just a wee comment, just something whatever it was and it was to do with 'people from the north'. Yet when she made it her hand was on my wrist and was stroking. That was a funny thing to do. How could she do that at the same time? What did that make me to her? I was just like a body. That was the dichotomy. You got it in philosophy about mind and body but this was out the sociology books where people were treated as bodies without a mind. She was taking me to her room anyway and we were trying to escape, that was what I thought. I did not know why we waited in that company or why we joined it in the first place. She must have liked them. That was her. It was up to her, it was her place and her friends. I was a stranger. I was a foreigner, a visitor from another planet, an alien, maybe I was invisible. Sometimes I was but not to her, and it was to her, I did not care about them, saying that or whatever they did, it was her, her doing it and at the same time stroking my wrist, she was, just stroking me, and it was just jeesoh if she wanted sex, the way she was stroking, people would have seen her, the way she was doing it to me. It was following from me, how I had stroked her, that was why she was doing it, she loved me stroking her and there in the cinema lying into me, she loved me doing it and just it was like hypnotizing and if she did it to me jeesoh it was just so – really it was amazing. There was not anything to say it was sex, really and what was there to say I just felt sometimes I was lost. I did not expect any woman to enjoy sex, not like the way a man does, it was a way the woman had of getting the man. If she set her sights on somebody that was how she done it, she used her body. We got seats away from people and did it to each other.

But she really did enjoy it. She said she really did, she laughed at me.

Maybe it was an acting thing. People say what they think. You just do not get liars, not like in the everyday world: that was what she said. I did not believe her. Actors were people and people were people, either they were liars, or they were not liars; and some were both. That applied to most people. Everybody, sometimes they lie and sometimes they tell the truth.

I read the play she showed me, just heavy and dark but to her it was the greatest. She was the first woman I knew who just wanted to have it, and like how I did, if we were sitting someplace like the tube or a bus or even in a supermarket or going along the street and she would touch me and what she wanted to do, just whispering jeesoh it made you shiver and if she touched me sometimes not even knowing it just touching me or brushing against me, her actual hand. She held it in her hand and just looked at my face; she did that. It was like a specimen. She did not know how I would react because she was a female and did not know about males, so if she touched it, seeing what I would do. Faint! That is what! She was seeing my face for the reaction. She was doing psychology and biology and it was like a biological finding, she said it for fun, if you squeeze him there what changes will occur in his facial movements, that was it, how will the male react.

But really I think it was girlish. I could see my sister doing that, and giggling. I thought of Celia as a woman but she was weeks younger than me. Really she was a girl. Was I good-looking? Maybe I was. Once my aunt called me a handsome boy. That was great. My mum scolded her for it. We do not want him swell-headed. But that would not have made me swell-headed, your auntie. I used to think I might be handsome, but then saw that I was not, not in comparison to other guys. They had better looks, or more popular ones. People would call them handsome without much thought whereas not me, if they called me anything, it would not be that but just you hoped they would look twice.

And I worried about stuff. Not that but other things, and if I was gay, sometimes I thought that. I did not like being at the same urinal and if guys washed their hands beside me I was just self-conscious all the time and did not know what they were doing and then if I blushed, just blushing all the time. It was just a nightmare. Celia called me a worrier. She was dead right. I worried all the time about stuff. A lot of it was nonsensical, absolute stupidity, just diabolical nonsense. Why did I worry about stupid crap! But I did, and looking for signs about everything. If you say that it means you are that. If you think that then it is a sign about really you are this. I was glad doing philosophy. I felt it was like 'oh calm down, calm down': that was philosophy. Rob Anderson saying about Socrates. Now, would you say that this was the case? Yes. And you would say further that this is the case? Yes. And would you also say that this too is the case? Yes. Then you are fine absolutely and must not worry, cannot worry, not about that, not about any of it.

I used to think I was happy-go-lucky but I was not at all happy-go-lucky.

But I had not thought I was a worrier until Celia said it. I was. Obviously. It was not a good thing to be. Worriers were geeky kind of guys. I never thought I was geeky. Maybe I was.

But she would never have gone out with me.

It was all just stupid. So what, if I was a geek.

Why trust her judgement? She was not always right. In relation to me I used to think she was but I was wrong. The trouble with me was I put her on a pedestal and you should never do that with any human being. My dad said that. He had been let down too many times, especially with union officials and people, politicians. It was something to watch for. They start off good guys then become right-wing bastards, selling out to the bosses, cowardly shits and money-grubbers, just careerists. It was like academics, how Rob spoke about them.

But it was not her judgement. She did not know everything. I knew she did not. The idea was ridiculous.

It was me, my fault. I thought that stuff. Nonsensical nonsense. Because I lacked experience. I was a naive idiot. That is the truth. It was just Celia, she had her own ideas, she went her own way. She did. That was a thing about her, it was a strong thing, she just made you smile, that was her. She was just I do not know except you were smiling, she made me smile because too of what she did, even thinking she knew everything. I was very very glad, very very glad, smiling to myself not even thinking about it, so I could smile, I could smile and I did, alone and in my own head, and it was an answer to her, so I was smiling and it was good I was smiling. I did not care, even about the future, if I got beyond it, I would, because it was the future, and how could you get beyond the future, it was impossible; the future becomes the present and the present is the past, the tortoise and the hare. I was the tortoise. I did not care, the tortoise is never beat and that was how I felt.

And the woman beside me, she was sleeping. That was trust. She trusted me.

I did not sleep. If only I could! I sat awake for hours. Unless sex, if it was after sex, I was always asleep until then I awoke, but I was ready, that was how I woke up, and if she turned into me it was just like hard again, it just made you shiver.

Out the window I recognized the skyline. So that was us, Glasgow in ten minutes.

The rain was not so bad now. It might even have gone off by the time we arrived in the bus station. It had to. I was not sure how to get home except by walking. I did not have enough for a taxi. Buses went from somewhere through the night but you waited for ages and you got trouble, especially on your own. Really, you were quite vulnerable. I felt that. I had not been home for a while. Probably it was just silly. Walking was okay if you went the main route. I thought that. Maybe I could have called my parents but that was a hopeless thing to do. My dad would have picked me up but I did not want him to. Anyway, I wanted to surprise them. They knew I was coming but not the actual day. I was going to do something like ring the bell and hide behind the wall. Boo!

But I was looking forward to seeing them. They would be the same. I appreciated my parents because of this. Things change. They did not. Other things in the world, relationships. I was coming home but where had I come from? It was strange. I felt very very strange. Not like at Christmas it was just a wee break, hurry home and hurry back. Not this time. Who was I coming to see anyway. Nobody. Parents and sister. Eric was a pal but at the same time, maybe I would not see him. There were other pals. Maybe I would see them. Maybe not. And who had I left behind. Nobody. It did not matter. It was my fault anyway. She did want to see me. She said she did. She said that to me. Although I did not believe her. Why should I? I was only one, one male. She had others. She had others. How could she have others? She did. But how could she have sex with other men if it was supposed to be me, if I was supposed to be her – not boyfriend, boyfriend was silly, if I had said the word to her, she would have thought it ridiculous and so very naive, and it would have been.

Maybe she was not having sex with them, any of them. Imagine I asked her. I could not.

I knew I was not special. I did not care. People said life was too short: did they even know what it was? It was like some of them never lived.

The bus was late into the station. I sat on while the other passengers got off. There was a queue for luggage. When I stepped down I saw my backpack, the driver had dumped it out and it was on a wet spot. Thanks very much. I lifted it and got it on and started walking, stepping my feet down hard because of tiredness and a kind of cramp.

Rain. Surely not. Yes. Although sometimes close in to a building you got drops falling. That was Glasgow, just walking along the street and you felt spots. It was like somebody was doing it on purpose, maybe out a window they saw you passing and sprinkled water down on your head. You could not believe they would do it, not to a stranger. Surely people would not throw water at strangers! Yes, they like a laugh. Even good people. Although how could they be good if they did bad things. Because they are people; people are people.

A strange thing about Celia was how she had a special name for herself to do with destiny and the stars. She got it from someplace and changed herself to it. She did not tell me what it was but it was how she saw herself. Something special lay ahead of her. It was there and she could reach out. She believed that. And for me too. I did not believe it. Well I did, but not for all people. She thought it was all people but how could it be, it was just stupid saying that. Maybe for her, not for everybody. Not me either, although maybe it could be. But not others, not ones I knew, like my parents and my sister. My family was not special except if something I did because it was me. If you asked them probably they would have said it was me, I was going to do something. But I did not think so. Only because I was at university but everybody was if they were middle class so did that mean they were all special? It was stupid thinking that. I was not special either, not extra special. I was not. I was just me, it was my life, and my life was ordinary, just nothing special at all. I knew that. Because I watched other ones and saw them. Maybe I would be a writer. I would like to be a writer because you could just be free and do what you wanted.

It *was* my life. Celia believed in other ones like in other religions people had all different lives, some better than others; it depended what you did in each; the better you did in one life the better the next would be. If you did bad things you became worse progressively, until you were not even a human being, perhaps you were a slug. Rob Anderson spoke about an ancient belief that was similar. Maybe it was the Egyptian epoch. There was good stuff to study next year. I quite fancied it, logic and stuff that took you to science, like physics, like how Aristotle was a scientist, that was what I thought brilliant, and I did not care.

Rain now definitely. A drizzle. The longer it went the heavier it would get. That was my luck, and I needed a piss. I did. That was stupid. I should have gone in the bus station. I just did not want to. And I thought it would make me walk quicker, if I did not, I would walk faster.

I had never been lucky with buses.

Our house was miles away and you could not get buses easily. Not in the evening never mind through the night. People took taxis or walked.

I had been trudging for a half an hour.

Life *was* unfair. It sounded childish saying it. Even the weather. It was as if the fates decreed it. And it was you. So you were the centre of the universe!

Celia believed that except it applied to everybody. We were all the centre of the universe. How did she work that out! It was almost beautiful but in a silly way. I challenged her on it. If it was a point to do with philosophy surely it was incoherent because if you think about Copernicus. She said it was a proper philosophical argument. But it was not, it was from religion and religion was naive. Most of it was or else just political like dad said, people getting power.

It was heavier rain than a drizzle. Had it been like this a while? Maybe. I was away thinking about things.

It happened to me. I could be walking someplace and forget where I was. I was so into my thoughts. I was not unique. Everybody is so none at all. Therefore why do we need the word? In the religions Celia respected all people were unique. But how could that be? Surely it meant the opposite of unique? Otherwise what does unique mean? It becomes worthless. 'Unique'. What do we mean by 'unique'?

That was Rob: 'what do we mean?' Everything was 'what do we mean?' I liked that. He was a real philosopher. He said he was not but he was. The way he worked out stuff put the other academics to shame. That was my opinion and I was not the only one.

Not Celia. If she had known more she would have had more respect. She thought she knew about philosophy but really she did not. I smiled at the things she said. Secretly she thought she was the true philosopher. She did! Maybe she was. Except in one sense, the one sense.

Even thinking about weather, what an odd concept. Changeability. Rain on your head. Imagine rain on your head. I stopped walking and looked upwards. You think of the weather and you think of God. Rain exists so must our Heavenly Father. How childish can you get. Religion is a childish thing.

Not quite childish. What? It did seem hard to believe. There is nothing wrong with 'hard to believe'. More like immature. People are entitled to find it so. And no wonder. Miracles! The worst aspect of 'miracles' was how it gave you the one individual. Miracles did not exist for everybody. That is what made it so childish. Catholics went to Lourdes and got cured of incurable diseases. Only them. God only did it for them. Oh it is a miracle for you and you alone! Not the chosen people but the chosen person. It was not conceited, it was nonsensical nonsense.

Absurd was the word. How could people think God
would do it for them and them alone, it was just so
childish. Childishly boastful. Oh I am cured. I had an
incurable disease but God cured me. It is a miracle and
He has performed it for me alone!

Why not everyone in the world who had the same
disease? As though God would distinguish the one individual. Why? Because you prayed! That was so conceited. God listens to one person's prayers. Surely
everybody who had the disease would pray for a cure?
Unless they were not Christians. But others would have
the same; an equivalent. Muslims would have an equivalent, and Jews, and other religions.

I am cured I am cursed. You only put in an 's'.

The backpack was quite heavy and I kept having to
shrug it up my shoulders. It was because I had brought
so much home with me. A subconscious manoeuvre in
case I did not return. Yet I brought the essays with me
so I was as indecisive as usual. In a comedy programme
on television the character shook his fist at the sky! I am
warning you God, just dont you mess with me. Rain,
sleet or snow. Dont you send that to torment me! Just
who do you think you are?

I went online and saw the original script, and the
original line was 'Who the hell do You think You are!'
But the television station would not keep it in. The producer or whoever said they had to take it out. Because
it was talking to God. Even 'fuck' would have been
preferable. Not so much preferable, but acceptable,
they would have allowed it, the BBC.

But 'hell'! How could you refer to God as in 'Who the hell do You think You are?' It was too much for them, as if it would have been too much for God.

The very idea of God worrying about something like that, it was stupid. And also conceited, just so arrogant and in a male sense too, very very male, I could see that, and Jean-Paul Sartre: Rob recommended him. He was very difficult but worth it.

But this rain; and needing a piss I did need a piss, really, I did. Why had I not gone, so stupid, when I had the chance. A little thing but out of little things.

Thinking about sex. That was you, you got paid back with a punishment. Needing a pee was a punishment for thinking about sex. The explanation was straight-forward. If you started going hard then soft then hard then soft no wonder you needed a piss. It was not a punishment. It was just natural, your body and bladder in a critical condition.

No point getting annoyed. Or depressed. More like depressed. The way stuff happens to one individual. Who else does it happen to!

Nobody.

Not quite true. Things do happen to other people. Me too. Some that happened recently were incredible. This was one more, one more I had to handle. I would handle.

Drizzle was not rain, it was like a sprinkling thing God threw down to help out the vegetables and plant-life, to give animals a drink.

Why was I talking about God all the time, given I was an atheist – agnostic at the very least.

Animals were out twenty-four hours a day, they did not have houses to go to and shops or cafés and even if there were shops and cafés they had no dough, they were completely rooked and could not pay for anything. That was me. Not quite rooked but nearly. Imagine being completely rooked! Not a sou, a penny or a cent. Nothing. What was fair about that? That was just so unfair. That was how unfair life was. No wonder people wondered. Some had fortunes, others had nothing. You did not have to be a communist to see that. I was not a communist and I could see it. Others did not. Celia only looked when I said it. Her family was not rich in her own estimation but actually they were loaded. Her mother was a doctor and her father was in business. Imagine saying that to my father: 'Honestly dad, her family is really not rich at all.' He would burst out laughing. What about mum, mum would just gawk, but she would smile too.

It was a different world. Down there people were rich. You did not know they were rich except eventually you came to realize it. An older student in Celia's tutorial group was an aristocrat or else maybe a cousin to one. Can you be a cousin to an aristocrat and not be one yourself? She and Celia were friends. When the aristocrat visited they had lunch in a local bar. Celia went too, just to see. He was tall and skinny and hardly spoke but he smiled at people and was not standoffish. He worked in 'the City' which meant 'stocks and shares and the movement of capital'.

Strange to think how this morning I was there and now I was here. Since it was after midnight it was not today but yesterday.

My parents did not have a big house but I still had a room and could coorie in for a few days; nobody to bother me; I could get on with the essays and just take it easy. I was quite looking forward to it. Maybe even I would stay in and not go out, not even bother seeing Eric or anybody for a beer. I quite sometimes liked essays.

At least I could relax.

Jees I was bursting and would have to find a place soon or else.

In my recollection this part of the city was hopeless. Even if there was a club bouncers were on the door, and they did not let people use the toilets; you had to buy something and be a customer otherwise 'eff off'. It was too late for bars. And the problem too was over-21. Bouncers picked me out. But it was illegal, so it was not their fault; only annoying if they let other people through and they were the same age. It happened with Celia all the time. It was females, they got away with it. Bouncers just let them in. Then if you did it outside and got caught. It was a real problem. But that was it and across the street was a lane. I walked over and along.

People did not like this area. Even rapes against males. Males raping males. There had been an outbreak of that. Not just young males. One had been in his forties. Imagine a guy of forty being raped! What did that mean? Who ever would do that? That had to be a monster.

I did not like the look of this lane. Some lighting but not much, so dark and shadowy, but that was good for the police.

The usual bins and old rubbish stuff. People just dumped things. You were scared to look down at where you were walking. Shit was the best of it. Then a spot that was better and I was able to unsling the backpack, just taking the opportunity, and what a relief to balance it on the ground a minute. You do not realize how heavy it is until you take it off and lurch a couple of strides. The straps would have left imprints on my shoulders.

Nearer into the wall jees I was bursting. My boots crunching on glass, then another noise. I heard another noise. A real noise, sounding like a woman and she was moaning. That is what it sounded like: 'oh no oh no oh no, no, no, no, oh no oh no.' Muffled and not too close. I waited a moment but it came again. Not a scream but moaning. I finished the piss and stepped aside, facing in that direction, staying still and listening hard. By this time my eyes were accustomed to the dark. A shape appeared and it was a man walking, heading this way along the centre of the lane; not too fast, coming along towards me. I started walking, acting normally, just keeping going, not hesitating and not too slow either, so not intimidated by him. But not to intimidate him either. Just not anything. He was approaching now he really was and he really had seen me. A thick-set man, older, oh fuck really heavy-looking too like a mafia gangster or something you could imagine him, and on he came. I would not confront him. How could I? Not here anyhow. Did I even know for sure it was him? I did not. He might just have been a guy, just out strolling.

Maybe he had seen something suspicious or if he heard her moaning. Maybe that was it and he just went up the lane to find out and here he was. On he walked down the centre of the lane, the crunching noise of his feet on the ground. Then he had passed. I wanted to look round to see him, to make sure he was not doing something behind my back. The way he had passed was like he had not even seen me. That was the way he acted, like he had not even noticed me. Even I was irrelevant. Maybe he thought that. Some older guys are like that, really arrogant the way they dismiss you. I kept on, walking in the opposite direction. I had to, that was what I thought. What else could I have done? It would have seemed completely strange. I could not look back. I would not tempt anything, although what could have happened? Nothing. No sound except my own. I would have heard, if somebody had been sneaking up. I would not have backed down. I had been in some bad situations in the past. I would not have backed down. I was not timid and nobody would have accused me of it, and not a coward, but not foolhardy and not silly brave. That was just stupid and helped no one. I was counting as I went, all to fifteen, and nothing, no woman, nothing. Maybe it was my ears. Ears play tricks. It was in all the books, your ears. Maybe they had. I was alert for anything yet nothing was there, all along the lane there was nothing. It was just dark.

Unless something had happened to shut her up. Ahead now was the end of the lane. On either side were weeds and a stack of rubbish bags. It was a place

where bodies were found, you saw it all the time; the
guy sneaking along with his girlfriend, looking for a
safe place for sex and suddenly there is a foot and it is a
leg twisted in the undergrowth. Call the police. Cold-
blooded murder. That was television. But such things
did happen. Maybe not much but definitely some of
the time, they did. Most murders were in the home
and the murderers that did it were known to the victim. It was not strangers you had to worry about it was
the next of kin, the person that stood to inherit, if you
were rich or even if it was insurance and if you were
just an ordinary person and oh my God almighty the
backpack, what kind of a fool I was such a fool, back
along immediately, but just a fool, just fast walking. It
had gone. Maybe not. I checked roundabout and everywhere, everywhere and everywhere all along, the edge
of the building, I could not believe what kind of a fool.
I was a very very stupid guy, very very stupid, just naive
and so stupid and just a total naive idiot. Could ever
I have been so daft! Never. Never ever. Never in my
whole life.

Sometimes if you were dead, only if you were dead.
People said that. I thought it myself.

Objects do not move by themselves, they do not
walk, backpacks do not walk.

I was not a headless chicken. My essays and everything else, books from the library.

Anyway, I could calm down and just look, look for
things, anything, calmly. Sometimes they get put to the
side, if somebody sees it, a lost article, if somebody

finds it, they put it at the side of the road, or like a glove or a scarf, they hang it on a railing so the person who has lost it can find it, so they retrace their steps and then they see the lost article.

I hunted around. Horrible bastard, dirty evil, just a horrible, horrible horrible. He would have been long gone. Probably someplace checking the contents, sorting through it all, maybe dumping stuff along the way, because it was just clothes and a lot of them were unwashed, and just old tee-shirts and stuff. That is what he would think. But some were good; especially the tee-shirts. It was not all crap, though maybe that was how he would see it, crooked coward. He would not bother about the books, or anything, essay notes, just dump it, they were not of value. There was nothing of value. What did he expect to find a bag of money! thousands of pound notes stuffed into plastic bags! People watch too much television, all these detective programmes. They go about seeing themselves involved in mystery dramas, the earphones in and the music playing, their music, people choose their own music, they do not choose the best songs, the ones that they like the very best, they choose the ones they see as soundtracks to their own sweaty lives. Pathetic. You saw them walking along the street, and even their voices, you heard their voices.

Unless it was for my benefit. If the woman was in it with the man and that was why she moaned like she had. Because that woman moaned I swear to God she really did. Really, she did. If so it was the very last time, never ever would I ever fall for such a thing again if ever it was a woman and she was in trouble, it would never ever happen again, that was me now, just finished. Imagine a woman and she did that moaning so people would be tricked.

I had stuff at home but it was for emergencies only; basics, old stuff. Even socks. My parents would loan me money, just give me it. If I asked. I would not ask. I would just sell something or else the pawnshop. They would laugh. Mum would be glad it was nothing worse. I would not tell them.

Except my essays and the books, library books, and where would I get them again.

I was at the top of the lane, and stopped. It was the second time I had reached here. I turned to stare back along, silence all the way, just nothing. I had to retrace my steps again. I did not want to, not again. But I had to. Although nothing would be there. My backpack was gone and the guy that took it, and the woman, if ever there was a woman, or just my ears playing tricks.

What else, but I just had to, just go back along the lane, that was all I could do because what if I saw it, it might be waiting for me right at the very end, I might see its shape, just sitting there waiting for me. How could I have missed it! How ever could I have missed it? It would be the strangest strangest experience ever and I would just get it up onto my shoulders and rush fast to get home, oh jeesoh, jeesoh, I so wanted home.

The Later Transgression

At this stage, when things appeared to be running smoothly, his transgression surprised me. Upon reflection it was no more and no less than I should have anticipated. His life may have been seen as one to emulate, to strive after or towards, but it was far from commendable. I knew that. He had not lived a perfect life. My friends respected him; young men like ourselves. It is safe to say that.

A companion of ours, a musician, did not survive though his existence exhausted itself in a similar way. When we three were together and smiling on how things had been, partly it was relief that we had survived at all. None among us pretended, none among us was the hypocrite.

In the ordinary ethical sense we had not lived just lives but nor had we pretensions toward the religious or theological sense of other existences, nor of existences yet to come. For myself I had no intentions of accepting a second existence. I grew weary of Lives to Come, a Life to Come, that Life to Come. As with our former friend I was one of many, content that those who follow should wield the baton.

Universals do not exist. There is no ethic, no code of morality, no moral sense at the inner depth of our being. From an early period I too was aware that the sensibility is unaffected by the violence or abuses perpetrated by one on another, even if the one is close to us. Yet I was perceived as ruthless. So too was our former friend. But did he fully understand what ruthlessness might amount to? Perhaps he did. When his grandfather died he rowed the boat that carried his ashes. His father and younger brother were seated at the stern. His younger brother unscrewed the receptacle and emptied the ashes midway across. His father could have stopped him. The following is hearsay, that he too could have stopped him.

Ingrained

I was not an artist and not a schoolteacher, I had never been a schoolteacher. People thought I was. That was a peculiar misjudgement. 'Misjudgement' *was* the word.

I was observing, even as I thought in this self-conscious, deliberately reflective manner, and the subject of my observation was the world about me. Here beyond the window, far below at ground level the rubbish piled high and overflowing although the rubbish men had come two days ago. What the hell had they been doing? All they did was stand there gabbing and sharing a smoke. Probably a joint; they pretended it was tobacco in case the rubbish police were spying from windows. I wanted to shout at them. It made me angry. Was that the way to do a job? Okay if it was a middle-class rural piece of suburbia but this was a slum man, a slum, s l u bloody m. Ordinary working-class people, these were brothers and sisters. We dont shit on them for heaven sake. So no wonder I got angry, living round here. It was just important. I thought so anyway, if no one else did. Lindsey did. Lindsey was shocked; truly she was. This was her first time in the city and the idea of bringing a baby up in such a place, my God. Where do the children go to play?

The same place they went when I was a kid.

Oh dont give me that, she said.

Give you what? I wasnt giving her a thing. It was true. All I did was tell her. If she chose to not believe me or to be annoyed by it, or be irritated; whatever, it was up to her. She accused me of being lev – lev – lev something. What the hell was the word! Levaticus? That was the name of a biblical character. Leviticus. She couldnt have accused me of being a biblical character? Or could she? It depended on her mood.

But it was no laughing matter.

People did not believe in laughs and she was no different. Neither was I. Laughs laugh laughter. I didnt believe in laughs either. That is why I returned to Glasgow, when any sane individual would have remained elsewhere, excluding Scotland obviously, if one might distinguish between the two, as most folk do.

The backcourts, backstreets, back alleys, the shadowy lanes nearby the river, derelict warehouses with caved-in roofs, broken glass and old iron, and weeds, and people; people who might be anything, dangerous, anything. That is where the children played, so what was new in that? Kids survive.

It wasnt my decision. I would have stayed south. I kept that to myself. Lindsey would have jumped down me throat, be entitled to jump down me throat.

Hoh hum.

Black soot ingrained brick buildings.

Black soot ingrained brick buildings, sandstone bricks, forming a rectangle. For every two entrance ways there was a midden containing three large metal containers inside of which piled black polybags full of rubbish and shite, shite. The containers should have been emptied weekly. They were not.

I would to have drawn them.

I adjusted the stub of charcoal between my fingers, my pinkie and ringfinger ached. The charcoal was finished and these two were the fingers that had the most work to do, thankless work. I should have thrown the stub away. If I hadnt paused to perform the adjustment the ache in my fingers would have gone unnoticed. A proper artist wouldnt have noticed. He would have been too engrossed. I was not a proper artist. I engaged in pastimes; this was one such.

When was soot anything other than black? It was always black. Soot was soot. No wonder I was having the difficulty. How do you draw soot you do not draw soot, who could draw soot, no one could do it, ever do it, they would never succeed.

Wait. Soot could be brown, soot could be purple. Soot need not be black, black grey. How do real artists manage? They just plunge in and try, they do not ask first; what colour is such and such; they just jumped in and did what it was, in front of their eyes, their eyes, theirs and nobody else, it lay in front of their eyes. What lay in front of their eyes? Whatever, what it was, whatever it was, and if it was green it was green, and why should it not be green, if soot is green it is green, fucking green!

I looked at the drawing, then out the window. A pigeon. One of the tenements lay derelict and a commune of pigeons had taken over the top flat. One landed exactly then, wings barely flapping. They flew in and out the broken windows, lined the juncture of the roof and on the chimneypots, digging their beaks into the moss-covered slates. Imagine worms on the roof. And hopeless-looking birds, but not in flight. The bigger the bird the more graceful it was, leaving aside pelicans. What was the wee fat bird that nests on these break-neck cliffs overlooking the sea? Not terns.

That was you getting old when your memory went. My uncle said it. Once the memory goes it becomes a downward spiral. They fly ten thousand miles without a break. Wee fat birds that the old St Kildans used to eat. These men climbed up incredible cliff faces in their bare feet because maybe only their big toe could find a grip. They had feet like shovels, with webbed toes, evolved from a thousand years of climbing. More. When had the first humans come to the island? Probably chased there five thousand years ago, same period as the Skara Brae settlers in Orkney.

Webbed toes! Surely not. How could it be? If they had had webbed toes the whole world would have known. Maybe they did. Anthropology was the appropriate area.

Life was just extraordinary. In some ways it was. Even you looked out the window, observing from the window, and saw the big puddle. Really, it was an enormous puddle. It flooded the entire backcourt and left all the families up two closes no way to reach the midden. Not unless they trailed through the water. Fucking webbed feet, ye needed webbed feet to live in Glasgow.

How to reach the midden? Send the weans!

What the hell else do we have children for? They would love the adventure!

But it was disgraceful; a scandal said Lindsey and she was right. Why should any child have to live in this environment. This place was horrible; infant mortality rates scandalous, scandalous; people living in confrontation with their surroundings, a pitched battle between the two, unlike what's his name, Lowry the great Lancashire artist who painted scenes from working-class life, crowds of people going to work in the factory, returning home from the factory. Lowry had been a political animal. He had to have been. Otherwise why use the subject matter?

I was not a political animal. This was a confession I enjoyed. I felt justified. Perhaps not. But it was a justification, whether I felt it or not. I liked to think I was political but I was not – my God, a bird had popped out the top window of the derelict building, out onto a windowsill, arms behind its back, beneath the coat-tails, head cocked, gazing down to the backcourt, supreme observer, a God-like witness.

But why the hell had they allowed the building to degenerate into dereliction? It was a nonsense. This city's political leaders, the ones that werent corrupt, were a bunch of cowardly bastards, no-good cowardly bastards. But it was up to the citizens to take up arms. Fight the buggers. Fucking fight them, dont be scared. Not that they were scared, they werent scared at all, they just had better things to do with their time, unlike me.

I was a do-nothing.

Like every place else on the globe, the battle in Scotland lay between the people and the politicians, the people and the political system, the class system, the people and the bullies, the people and the sycophants, the people and the armed forces.

Why not get actively engaged in politics. How to manage that? Go out and do something. Find a campaign and go and join it. People were fighting against racist laws. Go and join a picketline. Why was I unable to do that? Or Trident missiles, the people down at Faslane, young and old, elderly, all fighting against the army, navy and cops and the secret services, not to mention their American coozans, all down there fighting ordinary Scottish folk. Why didnt I go and join them? And take my child with me. People took their children. I didnt. Me and Lindsey, we didnt. If I suggested that to her she would run a mile. I never did suggest it, I didnt have to.

But who said I was unable to do it!

Unproven.

One day I might. One day soon. I had only been home a couple of months. Even being home was a surprise, never mind the accoutremon. Girlfriend and babee.

Life moved on. A lighter touch was required. Defective technique. One day I would seek tuition. There were leisure classes in the field. How to be an artist in ten weeks. It shore sounded good ol partner.

Yet the political activists were the ones to admire. Both my siblings were activists. I was not. But so what!

Here at the base level, street level, the level of existence, ordinary existence. My siblings didnt deign to stoop so low. I had the family, they had none.

That aspect of white crayon, its smoothness in application, no, I did not care for it.

Down in the backcourt dissolving lumps of excrement and tissue paper clogged the water. The flooding caused by three days' heavy rain and one burst pipe. The level of the puddle had risen to the extent that one now had to search for the source. What could one do. Very little. I dampened the white crayon with my forefinger.

Kids and adventure. On the dry land athwart the puddle they were building a flat wooden vessel. Call it an ark. These little humans were raising an ark to set sail for Treasure Island. Forget the religious connotation, the small ones were into Pieces of Eight Massir Awkins. You had to laugh. I did, I liked kids and having one of my own was beyond anything imaginable. Incredible that a human could bring another human into being. Of course Lindsey had played a part in the process. It takes two, two.

And where was the child to play. The backcourt was a massive adventure playground and I would have loved it when I was a wean, but now: now it was too dangerous. You could not let kids out there, not until they were older. Other parents did and I had no problem with that although Lindsey did. She was from the south seas of England and dint understand tenement life ol partner.

Neither did I.

On one roof across from me I could see two men working with slates and tarpaulin, repairing the recent storm damage.

That or a storm similar had struck the south-east coast of North America. Although the information was an irrelevance it helped people feel better. Nevertheless this here had been the worst storm for twenty years according to Mrs McAuley on the ground floor left; a crabbit woman who spent most of her life in the local butcher shop. Was that not unnatural behaviour? My father was a horse punter and spent most of his life in the betting shop which, if not admirable, was at least understandable. But butcher shops! There was something deviant about that. Every time one passed along the pavement and gazed into the butcher-shop window lo and behold that female personage was there at the counter, in conversation with the butcher's wife, Mary, a local tradition-bearer. Forget the word 'gossip'; 'gossip' did not do justice to the scope of what passed locally from mouth to mouth.

I was chuckling. I caught myself doing it. My thoughts delighted me. Yes and the toddler had returned in the backcourt below. Post haste. Red crayon red crayon. Nee naaawww neee naaawww. Red crayons for toddlers, certain toddlers. Definitely a red crayon for this wee being of the gender female with the spoon and cup

the spoon and cup

lost to the world making sandpies from out the black slime. The wee darling. I knew her mother and for God sake she was okay for all that never could she be described as a good mother. Never ever. She definitely was not a good mother. On this Lindsey and I agreed. As disinterested observers no other judgement was possible. She smoked like a chimney, went to the bingo, no doubt drank copious quantities of alcohol, to wash down the copious popped pills, all the while allowing her wonderful wee girl to toddle around this hellhole of a backcourt. What happened if she fell in the damn puddle; what if she fell on broken glass; if her flesh was sliced open? She would contract diphtheria. Nothing more certain. One felt like charging downstairs and lifting her out of harm's way.

But was she in harm's way?

Halt! Who goes there!

Middle-class missionaries.

Ah, pass on.

Artist as interventionist. The toddler in the puddle. I scraped an edge on the crayon, sketched quickly. Blunt crayons annoyed me unless appropriate. Appropriate crayons. How does one distinguish black-slime sandpies from sand sandpies? Weans dont why should adults? Might they be so distinguished?

By an understanding of the nature of 'essence'. What is 'essence' mine fuhrer?

The aeroplane overhead. Fasten seatbelts. A London flight. The wealthy business class, commuters commuting. I commute, you commute. Five minutes to land. Already on the final descent. Oh my ears a-poppin. Here is a boiled sweet. The stewardess on the side seat stares vacantly, knees glued together. Glued together. I was once on a plane and a stewardess sat so facing me. Her knees! It was a big plane and I was on the seat at an exit door. And travelling alone, though such information is not relevant. The stewardess sat on the pull-down seat facing me. And amid much turbulence and a most bumpy landing her knees remained together, dimpled knees, not beautiful but yes, well, maybe they were.

Are all knees dimpled?

But how did she manage it! How could it be! Mon amee! Such compo-zure! Such aispeer-yons! Such aileegons.

Needless to report she had nice legs. All stewardesses have nice legs. Given that the uniform skirt is not conducive, should not have been conducive.

I challenge that. They are so conducive!

But conducive or not, 100 per cent female, women's skirts. And what about her vacant stare? And could it be drawn. Hold it there a minute. Miss would you please be vacant a little longer. But why had I to unspread my own knees? Why! Why indeed, because I was getting hard. An erection occasioned, was occasioning, been brought about, effected by, the presence of these knees, and what and what, oh, what lay not so much

the knees of this woman, this stewardess whose stare was not at all vacant, or if it was yet concealing a most interested smile, a smile of daring, of daring – design!

Is design too strong a word?

The sense of the irresistible. Not by nefarious design aforethought, simply the non-reflective act of a free man. No no no. It was more than that. I was unspreading my knees for her, for her! She had been reading a magazine and pretended not to notice. And her knees my God stuck together, how could it be!

Now that surely was unnatural. Women surely are not programmed to keep those knees jammed together. Mine might be closed but not jammed. Hers were jammed. Jammed! Why?

Why indeed.

Now that had been unfair advantage. But the phrase 'vacant stare'. Perhaps that stare was not so vacant. Perhaps that stare was a stratagem. How to deal with male intimidation. And it was. I had desired that she notice my masculinity. It was true. Who knows, maybe she would slip her phone number into my hand as we departed the plane.

Men have that over women. The freedom to open one's legs. Not even in trousers will a woman open her legs, not like that, spread; spread knees. 'Spread knees' could be the name of an audacious new deodorant.

Had I been a copywriter. Mercy me. In the days when one travelled alone. One had yet to become a threesome. Lindsey and I had met but were yet to form a relationship. We had slept together. We had slept together. Sigh. One could only sigh. A reflective exhalation.

Sounds, what were the sounds. Banging through the wall. Who lived through the wall? Ye gods. The mystery of it, and to remain so; destined as such.

I heard this banging at odd hours. An old-fashioned author was required to make of that a mystery so dreadful, of such awe-inspiring

Oh my, more banging.

I focused closely on visual rather than aural matter.

In the backcourt parts of the ground had been cemented over. There were also dirt patches and here weeds blossomed. Bits of charred wood, remnants from the fire last month, strewn among rusted pushpram parts and holey bedspreads.

Jesus Christ a ragman! An actual ragman! I thought they had died out centuries ago! This guy! A fucking ragman! He was dragging a sack behind him and stopping every two or three strides to poke under articles. He was doing it on the off chance. Spoiled articles. Old newspaper or linoleum, it looked like linoleum. And his dog was there. That was odds on, a dog. Ragmen always had dogs. Oft times they were known as 'rag and bone' men. That would be the nineteenth century when bones lay about the streets in the name of God.

But I remembered those men from childhood, rummaging around for stuff, any kind of stuff, every kind of stuff. I hadnt seen one for years.

Mercy me he was going to leave! Hold it! Hold it hold it. Hold it hold it hold it.

The ragman stayed barely a minute. Three balloons for your coat and hat. Any bones? The dog sniffing at his heels. The dog had that hopeful demeanour one expects from the canine as opposed to the feline.

Two wee boys were watching all this from behind a dyke. They would have stones, were about to hurl said stones. The ragman had not seen them. Neither had his dog. This dog was mean. I hoped it would bark at them and chase them.

Nearby the empty space, where part of the dyke was demolished such a very long time ago. A section had collapsed and crushed a child. Why not say it. Killed the child. The child was beneath the dyke. Bigger children had climbed onto the dyke. I got the story from Lindsey who heard it from Mrs McAuley. The bigger children had run away after the 'accident'. In case they got blamed.

Accident! The word had to be challenged. It did not do justice to the fact.

None ever was adjudged culpable. Not anyone. A freak of fucking nature. Council business. People had demanded the dyke's demolition. Oh naughty dyke. What did they put it on Trial! Naughty naughty dyke. Then did the Council act.

I had a wee child. If such a thing ever happened, if it ever happened.

I had sketched this dyke on numerous occasions. What was there about that dyke? Nothing. Bricks and mortar a soul doth not own. Obviously not. Nevertheless, I sketched it.

Dead weans and old dykes, a traditional Glasgow story

The ragman approached the close entrance to the derelict tenement. Aha.

Just to see what was what.

The place was reeking! I could have told him. I had been inside it a fortnight ago. The concrete floor was rutted and wet, urine and shite, animal and human. The walls running damp, initials and dates knifed into the plaster, gang slogans on the ceiling. Empty buckie bottles and bricks and mortar, bricks and mortar, gen-yoo-oine bricks and mortar. I laid down the sketch pad and crayons, massaged the small of my back. The baby's nappy needed changing. I should have done it an hour and a half ago. Then I could have gone for a walk, pushed the pram. I quite enjoyed that. I did enjoy it. I enjoyed it a lot!

Now Lindsey was due home.

In the background the drone of the radio. It came from through the wall. This was *the* radio programme, every lunchtime *the* broadcast. Who could believe people listened to such nonsense? But they did, in their hundreds of thousands. This person or persons through the wall from us; one's neighbours, they listened to it on a daily basis. Probably I had seen them on the street. Ordinary people, no irregular habits, except this compulsion to listen to extraordinary crap. Was this not the most extraordinarily crap programme in the radio universe!

The door the door the door. The front door was being unlocked. I went quickly to the cot and lifted out the baby, sniffed the nappy and knelt to the floor, dragging across the waterproof changing mat, laying the baby aboard, still sleeping my God, amazing. The room door opened.

Hiya Lindsey! I said, surprised as fuck.

She peered at the wee one: Sleeping?

Yeh.

She smiled, taking care not to glance at what I had been doing. That was enough. To not glance. I attempted a smile but really, people doing that, very difficult, very very difficult. What is it about life, life can be so affected, and how it affects us.

Want a cup of tea? Lindsey said.

I nodded, because out the corner of my eye, what I was working on, it was just obvious, just getting closer, I just had to get closer. How could I get closer! Always the damn problem!

Black soot ingrained sandstone tenements formed a rectangle. For every two closes there was a midden containing three square metal containers which should have been emptied weekly.

Can soot be other than black? Yes, this had been answered. Soot is anything. I no longer had difficulty with that. Or did I! Of course not.

Yes sir I might have known the baby was awake. Lindsey was here and the nappy, just a new nappy, the baby was looking at me, big fucking eyes. I was aware that my stomach was something or other, that it was me, me to blame.

Death is not.

I was losing consciousness. I felt like I was, if I wasnt. On this chair, awaking, I was waking and there were words but the words made no sense.

She was beside me, thank God, thank God.

But the whirring! And a rapidity about everything.

That was my life. It pretended to progress but didnt. Unless all was progress. The stuff that took one back was another way forward. Progress or not progress? It was a problem for some. Movement, its possibility. All these wise and questing individuals who existed decades prior to Plato, to Socrates, to old Zeno himself.

But it was not my head it was hers. I could barely distinguish it in the dark. I sensed it more. But to sense something is to distinguish it by other senses.

What went on inside her head? Frequently I thought I knew but I didnt at all. Even to think I knew was arrogance of the intellectual order. The intellectual order of males. There was no other kind.

But I was arrogant. Nothing new there. To know what went on in another's head one firstly had to know what went on in one's own. That made sense but not for long. My own head appeared straightforward. I never had the need to think. My body moved and my brain followed. 'Twas ever thus.

I paid close attention to her fingertips, the lines there. Those lines on the human body, on the skin of a human being, these were unique and an identifying feature.

Her body brought a smile to my face. It seemed as per a norm. What does that mean, as per a norm? It sounds insulting yet rang true. It connected to the human norm, she was as per the human norm. She was a normal human being, unlike myself. But I was a God. How else to describe myself? It was no egotistical feature, just the reality of my existence. It is said that each of us is God [a God]. This has become clear, it has been so since the birth of my children. I watched them grow and in their early months, these first couple of years, it was never more clear. And yet, and yet now, now at the present time in my life I see something amiss, is amiss, amiss with the argument.

I made a gulping sound; she was reaching her hands out to me, and picking up things, giving me other things.

Her throat also.

And my throat. I saw it when *I* shaved. The adam's apple. What use had my own throat been lately. And why think of myself? I returned always to myself. It was at the nub of the failure. But what was the failure? I knew. If I could not answer such a question, and only such a question, if I could not answer it then I must somehow answer the questioner who will want to know the effect the problem has brought about, given that it is the questioner who sets the question, and the question is the problem. Or so I thought, but it has become apparent that the question only becomes a

problem in relation to me, that in one most acute manner I am the problem.

Her pinkie reached out from the safety of her fist
which had been clenched, but not so tightly, otherwise
how could this movement of her pinkie have occurred.

It must have been a summer's morning. I was shivering. This should have been a source of amusement. For
myself, irony had been so very important, a means to
survival. My blood was so very thin. Yet I was fright-
ened to swallow a late-night brandy. I chuckled.

Here, she said.

What for me?

Yes.

It was her after all. No wonder I smiled. I asked was
it another sweater. No, she said, it is a cup of tea.

I heard her chuckle then her hand was to my forehead, smoothing; and to my temple.

She brought me presents. She laid them next to me.
One had been a sweater. I remembered it clearly. I had
not requested the sweater but had wanted one. Then
she was laying it beside me.

I said to her that I had not known I wanted the
sweater. But you knew. You knew. I didnt even know I
wanted it.

Oh but I saw ye were shivering, she said and laughed.

She saw I was shivering. Who then was the God?

But her laughter!

Gods cannot laugh. It was because I had answered.
She liked it when I answered. When I did not she became
depressed. She thought I was dying. I was not dying.

Recently I had been unable to answer. I wanted to answer but could not. I wanted to explain to her that I did not not answer intentionally. I did not care about the others. Only her, and even to her I found that I could not answer. I was ill-equipped, to speak. I could but would not. I was never speaking in a natural manner. I was not a useful person. I could not push myself. I listened in silence, prior and beyond, and preferred it so. I hoped the others would stop visiting. I cannot name them. This would be painful, for them.

I was an awkward patient. These were visitors who expected the visited to do the entertaining.

They had nothing to say and I had become incapable, of it.

What could I say to people, only speak when spoken to. Not reply.

My mouth opening, sounds issuing. They would listen and make sense of the sounds. People do listen.

It is true that she never did. She heard but refused to make sense of the utterances.

The faces of people reveal worry. I no longer opened my eyes.

She did not allow herself to be affected, and by not listening, by not listening

Are ye sleeping? she said.

I kept my eyes closed, eyelids closed. Yet tiredness had engulfed me, my God and engulfing, whatever engulfing

distrusting words too

Words used to be reaching, we were groping, human beings making use of words as a way forwards, it was progress towards, a progress

even could I be backwards, a groping towards a return, I was returning and seeking its continuation so that along the road my mind would numb

What eternity may be. I could drift, drifting. If I would lose consciousness, no.

Fingernails and zips.

I moved towards unconsciousness, the body being dragged, mind so being dragged. Yet when I revived, and was revived; fitly, I was fitly

How to stagger, which also is movement. I sought movement, I might stagger. A God could not stagger. My body. The stagger as an effect. How may there be effects of one's body, affecting oneself, affects on one's own body, effects of oneself

How would I speak of my death to her, speaking to somebody of that. Death is not, is not, isnay

What could I say to her, death is not, it is nought. Death is not really, it isnay

To her I could say it and not to others, it ended for them before that.

The Third Man, or else the Fourth

It was perishing. Ice on the ground, ice on the puddles. When ye moved yer shoes crunched. There was supposed to be horse racing this afternoon but anybody with half a brain knew it would be postponed. The ground was bone hard. Nay racing since last weekend. Not postponed: cancelled. Why not tell the truth. Ye cannay postpone an actual day, ye cannay put back a day, that would be like two days in a oner. It is not possible. What happens is the day gets cancelled, the day's racing; they just cancel it, the powers-that-be. Unless a big race is on the card; the Grand National or something, then they do whatever it takes. Otherwise no.

Jesus christ but it was bitter, a right cauld snap. It must have come down from the Arctic. We were standing there chittering. The conversation petered out a while ago, we were just keeping warm. Then we drifted off to look for burnables. Drifted is the wrong word but naybody said nothing when we went, we just went away, away by ourselves. I noticed that. It was almost weird the way it happened, like telekinetics or whatever the fuck ye call it.

There were three of us there at the time and then another one came and that makes four, so four of us. Whatever we found we stowed to the side of the fire.

Me, Tim and Nicky Parkes. Arthur was the fourth one along. That was us: the auld team. Nay point saying different. There is young teams and there is auld teams. Ours is an auld team. How do ye tell the difference? Because we dont tan the bus shelters, no like those little toerag bastards.

The Council put up a new bus shelter yesterday morning. At five o'clock yesterday afternoon it was caved in, glass all ower the pavement. So how are dogs and cats meant to walk? They never think of that. Piles of shattered glass cutting into animals' paws, or else weans. And what about elderly people? Some auld dears come out without their shoes, they just wear their slippers, slipping down the stair for a couple of rolls and a pint of milk, they dont bother putting on their shoes, so these slippers with soft soles, fucking glass goes right through them and cuts their fucking feet.

That is these fucking hooligan bastards. I have nay time for them.

I never saw the new bus shelter myself, before or after, it was Arthur told us. I was gony go along the street to have a look. Wound up I didnay bother. I had somewhere to go. What interests me but is their fathers. Who is their fathers? the wee toerag cunts. Naybody knows. Ye hear guys talking in the betting shop or the boozer and they all shake their heads, all annoyed. If they could get a grip of the wee bastards! They say stuff like that. If they were my boys!

Well who the fucking hell's boys are they? Know what I mean. Nay cunt owns up! Ye never hear anybody going, Oh him, that wee fucking toerag, my youngest!

Naybody says that.

They must all be orphans. It would be a different kettle of fish if it was getting signed for a football team. Oh my boy my boy! Kilmarnock just signed him on a full-time contract. The Hibs have offered him terms.

Then they would be rushing to claim them. Ye ask me it is hypocrisy. I have nay time for it. I hate that vandalist anti-social stuff. Ye try to keep a place as best ye can. It is us that use it. If ye want to vandalize the place go to Kelvinside or Newton Mearns, Bearsden – someplace the rich cunts live.

My own boy was past the stage. But he never done it anyway; no even when he was that age. Me and the guys were talking about it. No question. I would have punched fuck out him, that one of mine.

What about yer wife? said Arthur. Would she have let ye?

What ye talking about?

Does she no mind if ye hit him?

Well I dont hit him now Arthur he's fucking thirty-seven.

Arthur nodded like he had scored a point. I looked at Nicky Parkes and Tim. They were listening. Tim was rolling a smoke.

Of course she minded, I said, she's a woman int she!

Arthur shrugged, blew into his cupped hands and rubbed them in front of the fire. That annoyed me. He annoyed me.

Forget it.

I looked at the fire instead. It was going good. The last pile of burnables included a wooden cupboard thing that Nicky Parkes dragged ower from behind the shops. Me and Tim broke it up. If we had just pitched it on it wouldnay have lasted as long because of the draught catching in under the spars. Yer fire just goes up in smoke. An old story but a true one. Some people know about fires, other ones dont. Arthur for instance. Mind you he liked a heat. He never done nothing for the fire but loved heating his hands. He just stood there rubbing them. It grated on me. Then he made comments about yer family! What a cheek! Families are taboo. Naybody should interfere with that. What the hell did it matter to him what my wife said about my son? Sons are boys and boys are boys. Ye know what women are like about boys, I said.

Arthur squinted at me like he didnt know what I was talking about.

Sons, I said, they're their pride and joy.

The fucking sun shines out their arse ye mean. Arthur shook his head and spat into the fire. A different story when ye're merried to them, when the boy grows to a man. Fucking nag nag nag.

Discipline begins in the home, said Tim, looking directly at me. Or not at all. Tim was licking the gummed edge of his roll-up. He smiled. It was you said it.

Me?

Aye.

What did I say?

Ye would punch fuck out him. Yer boy, if he went to the hooligan games.

Well so I would. When he was that age. Know what I mean, it's a long time since he was a teenager.

Tim smiled again, eyes closed and shaking his head. He had a habit of doing that. It was fucking annoying, like ye had said something daft. Why not come out and say it, if that was how he felt. I saw him gie a wee look to Arthur but I didnay say nothing. Him and Arthur could gang up on folk. We were all mates but some were matier than others. It was like that in this world. Since time immemorial. It gied ye a pain in the neck. If ye let it get to ye. I didnay. We cannay be everything to everybody. Nay point trying. I learned that a long time back. It was just that I talked too much. Sometimes I wished I didnay, I wished I could shut up, just shut my fucking mouth.

Nicky Parkes was like that. He hardly said fuck all and was the better for it.

Tim had made him a roll-up as well as one for himself. He got the light from the fire. He didnay have to because him and Tim both had lighters. But it was good using the fire. Same with me if I had smoked. It saved ye lighter fuel as well. But it was more than that. Ye just liked doing it. And then the smell, I aye liked the smell of fires, even auld yins; the smell on yer hands.

We watched Nicky Parkes getting the light. He tore a page out a newspaper and folded it lengthwise. Lengthwise! That made me smile. And it was very tight the way he folded it; ye might say crisp. Deep and crisp and even. When he had it burning he held it for Tim. Tim had to draw his head back in case the flame burnt up his nose and eyelashes. That was close! he said.

Once they had their lights Nicky Parkes dropped the paper on the fire and we watched it flare up then settle; burnt out, the ash blowing. There was a wee swirl of draught roundabout this place, and ye felt it. I did and so did the other three. Auld age; the blood gets thin. Too many fucking aspirin. Imagine the chemist firm that made them went bust, and they stopped manufacturing the cunts: half the male population of Glasgow would collapse with heart attacks. I was going to make a comment on the subject but couldnay be bothered. Tim started telling us about an auld cunt that froze to death. It was in the *Evening Times*. Nayn of the rest of us had read about it. Froze to death in Scotland! It was hard to believe. All kidding aside, he said. It was a gaff in Miller Street.

There's nay gaffs in Miller Street, I said, nay cunt lives in Miller Street. No nowadays, it's all shops and offices.

We're no talking nowadays.

All I'm saying is naybody lives in Miller Street.

Right enough, said Arthur.

Tim sighed. I'm no gony argue the point. It isnay me saying, it, it was in the *Times*. They found the auld guy deid; they had to batter down the door and it was a tenement building down Miller Street

A tenement building down Miller Street … I shook my head at that. I thought they were all offices.

They are all offices. Was it upstairs or down? said Arthur

Tim glared at us. How the fuck do I know.

It matters.

Matters fuck all, yez are just being stupid.

It matters if ye're trying to work it out, said Arthur, that's all. I'm no trying to get at ye.

Tim sighed.

Did they say where they found him?

I dont fucking know, wait til I phone them.

Naw, said Arthur, likely it was a basement; down a dunny. They auld tenements are full of dunnies. That's where the auld yin will have been staying. The same round the Clyde walkway. It's all manholes and dunnies along there. The homeless go down at night; they've got saunas and fucking tv lounges down there. Know what I mean, they homeless cunts, they've got better conditions than us, better than Barlinnie. Maybe the auld yin done the same, climbed down a manhole and got lost!

Shoosh, I said, I cannay go this right-wing shite.

What d'ye mean? Arthur grinned. It might be shite but it isnay right-wing.

Of course it is: Hate the Homeless week yet again.

Gie us a break.

It was a joke, said Tim.

Aye joke the coalman.

Tim shook his head and dragged on his roll-up, blew out the smoke. He gazed across to the back of the shops. There was a big black dog sniffing about at a pile of bricks. Some size of a dog, he said.

Nicky Parkes was looking at it. I'm fucking starving.

Dont tell me ye'd eat the dog? I said.

Fucking right.

I wonder how come it's sniffing about there? said Tim. Probably a deid body buried under the ground.

Think so?

Oh aye.

Mind you, said Arthur, it is feasible.

I turned and spat a gob into the fire. It sizzled a moment.

Arthur said, Careful.

What do ye think it's going to put the fire out?

I didnay mean it like that.

Aw, okay. I nodded, but in a sarcastic way. Arthur annoyed me. He knew he annoyed me. The cunt couldnay make a fire and here he was taking control.

It was me and Nicky Parkes made the fires. Tim helped but no that much. But it didnay matter. I liked making them anyway. I am no saying ye have to be special to make them. But what I will say is: some folk are good at it.

Same when I was a boy. We used to set fire to fields and all sorts, middens and what have ye. We set fires everywhere. There was a rubbish pit no far from our street and we dragged stuff from it. I am talking childhood days, the bygone era. Ye learned about fires. Leather furniture for instance, ye learned about that. Some stuff is dangerous. Motor-car tyres. Rubber. If that lands on yer wrist ye know all about it. Burning rubber; I once got it on my legs. There is more to fires than people think. Nicky Parkes was the same. I knew it the way he built them. And ye have to build them. Fires, I said.

The other three looked at me.

Ye've got to build them. I'm talking if ye want them to last.

Oh aye ... Tim glanced ower at Arthur.

Nicky Parkes was shaking his head. No at me. He was away thinking about something else. He was even staring in another direction. He was a rude cunt at times. Ye were standing with him but he was away someplace else. How come he palled about with ye? Ye wondered. I liked him but. I dont know why. But I did. He drifted in and out of company. Now ye see him now ye dont.

Like the auld guy, him that died; freezing to death inside a cold tenement building, nay heating or fuck all. What a life. Ye thought ye were doing okay and then ye werenay, ye woke up fucking dead, a block of ice. Poor bastard. Probably he had grandkids too.

The auld yin? said Arthur.

Aye.

Arthur nodded. That's what I was thinking.

Poor auld cunt.

Heh Tim, what did the headline say?

Man found dead.

Man found dead, it hardly fits the bill. No for something like that, said Arthur, fucking tragedy.

Tragedy's right, said Tim.

I said: Scandalous. Scandalous is the word I would use.

Nicky Parkes was watching me, he was expecting me to say something more. What? What was I supposed to say? There wasnay a single solitary word. Poor auld cunt, what a way to go. It just wasnay fair. That was the world for ye.

I stepped sideways and edged some burnables into the fire. At least we had a fire. Unlike the auld yin. The truth is I didnay like Tim's story. I was even half-prepared to know his name. Almost like I knew I would. I asked Tim. Did they gie ye his name?

Him that died?

Aye.

Tim thought about it. Naw, he said.

I shook my head. There was just something about it, some familiar thing.

What do ye think ye knew him?

Naw I mean, nay reason to think that, nay reason at all. Except just

What?

I dont know …

Arthur started speaking about something. The other two listened. I didnay. I rubbed my hands at the fire. Thank fuck it was going good. Sometimes they didnay.

Arthur was on about the time he did in Barlinnie. Ye were sick hearing about it. Some asbestos scare. Burst pipes in the cludgie ceiling. Or Gents' pisshouse as he called it. Gents' pisshouse! As if there was another one for Ladies! Barlinnie fucking Prison, know what I mean. The pisshouse was down the back of the block and down a step, and there was a slope there. The plumbers were in working. Ye went for a piss and came out looking like Santa Claus. It was all clouds of asbestos dust, that white fibre stuff. All the bears went on strike, said Arthur. A couple of laggers were in with us, they knew all about it. The screws were feared, they werenay gony do fuck all until we telled them! They were going, Dont worry about white it's blue that's the killer! A load of fucking keech. White's every bit a killer.

Too true, I said, there's brown, white and blue; each one of them's deadly.

That was what we said, go for a shite and ye're a goner. Know what I mean, ye're in for Breach and wind up it's a death sentence, mesotheli-whatever-the-fuck.

Christ! said Nicky Parkes.

Stories about the jail aye interested Nicky Parkes. It was obvious he had done time. He wasnay the brightest of cunts but he was crafty. I yawned. It wasnay that jail stories bored me but I had heard this one afore: no just from Arthur.

I stopped listening. He was in full flight. Governors and ministers and priests and fucking royal princes or some shite. What next man the three fucking stooges.

The thing about the asbestos story, I didnay know what it *meant*. It must have *meant* something. Otherwise how come guys telled ye about it so much? Was it like solidarity between screws and bears? There was something like that the way Arthur telled it. Fucking shite.

I drifted, looking for stuff.

Ye done time in there ye wanted to forget about it, ye didnay go yapping about it every ten minutes. That was what I thought.

I found a wooden contraption, like a wean's playpen or an old-fashioned chute for toddlers maybe. I propped it up on a couple of bricks and stuck the heel on the uprights, snapped them easy. I kicked them ower to the side. It definitely wasnay a chute. Nicky Parkes came ower to help and we kicked it nearer the fire. Good wood, I said. All we need is a carton of coffee and we'll be well away.

What about a wee brandy?

Exactly, smoked salmon and a pound of grapes.

Now Nicky Parkes gave a look in the direction of Arthur. I just shrugged. These two never saw eye to eye. I stayed out it. I didnay get on too well with Arthur either. There wasnay many cunts I did get on with. The wife said that. I was a crabbit auld cunt. That was what she called me. Well, she didnay say cunt, she didnay like swearie-words.

The word for Nicky Parkes was moody. Ye didnay want to do him a bad turn. It was him and me kept the home fires burning.

He had the touch. Ye notice that with fires. Same as a boy, when you and yer mates are building a fire, when it comes to lighting it, getting the thing going, it is usually just the one or two that does that. The other boys stand back. I was quite good. I have to say but something tells me I wasnay in the Nicky Parkes league. Just something about him.

And oily cloots werenay needed either. It wouldnay matter if a galeforce wind was blowing. One match, that was all he needed. He would burn down an entire leisure complex, hotels, fucking restaurants. He was yer man. He was smiling at something. Hey Pat, he said.

What? I said.

A large brandy would be better than a wee yin.

Yeh.

He laughed: A large brandy waiter!

I laughed too. Plus a salmon sandwich!

Arthur looked across at us, wondering what we were laughing about. Meanwhile Tim yakked on about something.

It was about a guy had odeed. Who gives a fuck: that was what I thought. Drugs and dope, I cannay be arsed with it. That many problems in the world. Get us a winner at Cheltenham, that was what I was looking for.

But where was he? said Tim.

What ye talking about?

Him that odeed. I'll tell ye where he was man he was sitting on the fucking chanty, that was where they found him. Odeed on the fucking chanty, poor cunt.

A common scenario, said Arthur.

Is it fuck.

It is.

Tim glared at him.

I'll tell ye how.

Ye'll no tell me how. Tim cleared his throat, spat in between his feet and took out his tobacco again.

Nicky Parkes squinted across at me. It was because the other two were at the argy-bargy; usually they were on the same side. I couldnay care less, edging the wood to the fire. But I raised my eyebrows a wee bit. No too much. I wasnay wanting involved. All these battles. I would have been as well sitting home with the wife. I listened to Arthur and Tim for another couple of minutes then I shook my head. Sitting on a chanty but, what a way to go! At least it was a relief, I said.

That stopped them and they laughed. Usually I was nay good at jokes. This time it worked. Even Nicky Parkes was laughing; a kind of laugh. Ye never knew with him. He wasnay huffy or fuck all he just – I dont know. It was a strange kind of laugh he had; all this talk about cludgies but the truth is the laugh he had sounded like constipation grunts.

It wasnay his fault. Ye just had to be careful with him; that was what I thought. He stepped away from the fire now, turned his back on the company and off he went. Soon he was out of sight. That was Nicky Parkes. Not a fucking word of explanation. I watched him go.

Arthur had been chipping bits of stuff into the fire. Now he started telling us about a dream he had had. Jesus christ man. I checked my watch. Still too early; the doors hadnay opened.

Dreams by fuck! That was scraping the barrel. All ye could do was sigh. Naw but it was really weird, said Arthur, I was up a high road and I bumped into some-body close to me, I cannay mind who. It might have been one of yous cunts.

Gie us a break, I said.

Naw Pat seriously. Whoever it was, we're standing there and he's talking but it is the way he's talking, like he's excited, know what I mean? and nervy, dead nervy. I couldnay quite get what he was saying.

Hang on a minute, what are ye talking about?

A dream I had. This guy, the way he was talking, it wasnay making any sense. No to my head anyway. It was like my ears heard what he said but no my head. It didnay make sense, it wasnay getting through.

Ye talking about yer brains? I said.

Arthur looked at me but he knew I was serious. I dont know, he said, it was like my head but no my brains, once it hit my head it still had a way to go, if it was gony reach my brains.

Me and Tim looked at each other.

Arthur muttered, Nay comments ya pair of bastards. Another thing about him, the guy I was talking to, he was not a likeable person.

So who was it? said Tim.

It's difficult to say. It was all hazy.

Right.

Another thing was how he was trying no to laugh. I got that feeling about him, he was a nasty fucker.

Well that could be anybody, I said.

Arthur smiled.

I spat into the fire. There was something about him smiling that I did not appreciate. If there was a nasty fucker in the company it wasnay me or Tim. And Nicky Parkes had vanished.

Dreams are funny, said Arthur.

Oh are they? I said.

They can be.

I nodded, gieing Tim a look but Tim was all ears for the story. He was one of these guys ye could sell him anything. A good yarn and that was him. Where do I sign, show me the dotted line.

And Arthur could spin them, nay doubt about that. On he went: There was a wee lane going down the side, he said, like the one round the back of the shops along there, and the guy I've met is pointing to one of the back closes running along.

Round the back of the shops? said Tim.

Precisely. That's where I'm talking about. The back closes came out onto the lane so the front must have been round on the main drag. I am only surmising that cause ye know what like it is when it's a dream man ye dont fucking know I mean no for sure.

Hazy, I muttered.

Aye.

Ho man! Tim rubbed his hands, waggling his shoulders, enjoying the tale.

So anyway, says Arthur, along comes this other guy.

Other guy? I said.

Aye, and I know him, I know him well. So does the nasty fucker; in fact the two of them are mates, only I dont quite know who the first yin is.

What d'ye mean?

They get mixed up. I cannay mind who's first and who's second. That's the funny thing about it, I cannay remember.

Sounds like a load of fucking keech.

Arthur shrugged.

How many guys again?

Just like I says.

What, three?

Aye.

Could it no have been four? I said.

Arthur frowned. It was three, there was two then the third man came along.

The Third Man! said Tim.

No the fourth? I said.

Naw, said Arthur. That's the thing about dreams, everything gets slippery. One minute ye know the next ye dont. Weird.

Arthur smiled again and reached down to lift a stick from the ground. He used it as a poker, poking it into the fire. He dragged out half of something and kicked it ower onto its side, using the stick to shove it back in. I wished he would stop messing about. He didnay know about fires. Sometimes I get a daft feeling, like as if they know who it is made them; they will do what you want but if another cunt starts messing then who knows. Fires can be scary. I was about to speak when lo and behold Tim passed me a beer, a beer. A fucking magician! Where the hell did ye get that! I said.

Hch heh heh.

Ya cackling cunt ye!

You're getting auld.

I looked at him and the can: How did ye open it without me noticing?

Tim winked.

Seriously? I said.

I am fucking seriously.

Did ye drink out it as well? Ye couldnay have, I would have noticed.

Tim laughed; Arthur with him.

Pair of bastards, I said, raising the can to my lips.

Sip it now Pat. I've only the one.

Sláinte. I swallied a long mouthful.

Gracias very much, muttered Tim.

I passed the can to Arthur. He was about to take a sip when the three of us spotted somebody in the distance: Peter Craig, he was cutting through the gap site at the other end of the waste ground. He waved ower to us. Arthur shifted the way he was standing to hide the can of beer. Know what I mean, he said, that could have been the polis; open-air drinking, a major act of criminal magnitude.

I was still looking ower to Peter Craig. He must have smelled the beer, I said, imagine smelling the beer.

Tim retrieved the can from Arthur and swigged a mouthful. He swigged another then passed the can to me. I took a long one and passed it to Arthur.

Finish it, said Tim.

Arthur did, then crushed it to death with his fist. He got the stick and scraped a space for it near the middle of the fire, chipped it in and poked stuff ower the top of it.

Ye wouldnay mind if it was a bottle of malt, I said, but one can of beer. A hunner fucking yards!

Tom sighed and gied a mournful look. I hope he doesnay tell Nicky Parkes.

Say ye found it, I said, it can happen.

Arthur winked: We'll just deny it.

Right …

Aw man, I said, I feel pished. It's all this excitement.

Tim was puffing smoke. I mean it's no as if it was intentional. I just forgot. If Nicky Parkes says something, know what I mean, I wasnay keeping him out, I hope he wouldnay think that.

Not at all, I said, one can of beer and four mooths; one swally and ta ta.

Exactly, said Arthur. I wouldnay worry about it. Hey, I'll finish the dream.

Dont bother.

Naw but it's funny.

I'm no into dreams, I said.

Neither am I, but this one is different. Arthur winked at the two of us. It's got sex in it.

Aw for fuck sake.

Sex! said Tim, a big smile on his face.

This gets worse and worse, I said, and I spat into the fire again.

Aye but it's weird sex, said Arthur.

What a surprise.

Weird sex … Tim laughed for a moment but then he looked at me.

I said, What ye looking at me for?

I'm no.

Aye ye are.

Naw I'm no.

But he was. Then Arthur winked and it was me he was winking at. How come I don't know. Just be careful, I said.

What about?

Just be careful.

Ye're staring at me Pat, what ye staring at me for?

Staring at ye?

Aye.

I shrugged. Just dangerous territory man know what I mean, sex.

You're para.

I'm just saying …

Arthur shook his head and looked away.

Tell us anyway, said Tim.

Arthur waited a moment. I gied him the nod and off he went. But something puzzled me about it. My hearing was no as good as it used to be but that didnay mean I heard things that werenay said. That isnay what folk mean when they say they have hearing problems. I might have been deaf but I definitely was not eh

Paranoiac is the wrong word. I couldnay think of the right one. That was Arthur and his fucking yapping, yap yap yap. Tim was puffing on his roll-up, gieing that contented look he aye gave when somebody was telling a story. He must have been some wean. Ye could have sent him to sleep with a paragraph. Once upon a time the three bears – and then he would have been snoring.

Uch well. I prepared to listen. Come what may Arthur was going to tell us the story. There were times I thought conspiracies were on the go and they werent, it was only me. Two slugs of beer and I was drunk as a fucking skunk. The wife said that about me, alcohol made me paranoiac. I aye thought things were happening and they werenay.

Dreams bored the arse off me. I never told mine to cunts so how come I had to listen to theirs?

Mine were boring as fuck. That was when I got any. I couldnay remember the last time. They were so boring they never registered. I got dreams where nothing happened. Nothing at all. The dream opens and there I am strolling down the street. Oh I think I see a bus! And then the dream stops. Big deal, seeing a bus. Thank you God.

Imagine telling somebody that.

It wouldnay matter if Arthur's dreams were boring or no he would still want to tell ye them. The cunt aye had to be talking, just like the fire, he aye had to be poking the thing, messing it about. Yap yap yap, on he fucking went. Then in the distance: Nicky Parkes! He was carrying a polybag. Trouble, I said.

The other two saw him. Arthur quickened with the story, all about this nervy guy he met down the lane, turns out he had just had his hole. That was in the dream. Was it the punchline? I dont know, I wasnay listening. But Arthur was looking at me like he expected a round of applause. Is that all you can think about, getting yer hole? I mean what age are you!

What has age got to do with it?

Aye ye're well named, fucking J Arthur.

Cheeky bastard. What's up with you?

There's nothing up with me, I said.

The two of them were looking at me.

Nothing up with me, I said.

Grumpy bastard, muttered Arthur.

Tim was frowning at me. The man's got a point.

I dont fucking give a fuck about his point. I'm chittering standing here, it's fucking freezing fucking cold. I spat into the fire, slapped my hands the gether, turned to see Nicky Parkes arrive. When he did he opened the polybag and brought out a six-pack.

Pure astonishment.

He broke the cardboard, tossed us each a can. Arthur dropped his in the excitement, then moved to clap Nicky Parkes on the shoulder.

Tim was laughing, snapping open the can. Ya fucking dancer! he shouted.

Well done Nicky Parkes, I said.

I tapped a five, he said.

Who off?

Nicky Parkes patted the side of his nose.

Fair enough.

Tim had the tobacco out and was rolling the two of them a smoke.

Maybe I should have got a bottle of wine, said Nicky, that is what I was wondering.

Aw naw, the beer's great.

Aye but Pat I might have got fucking two: buy one get one free.

Oh.

A can of beer is a pleasure, said Arthur.

A pleasurable experience, I added.

That's right, said Arthur, and it provides a basis.

I looked at the fire and at Arthur and Tim. Somebody needs to get burnables.

They looked at me.

I got the last lot.

Did ye? said Arthur.

I dont remember that, said Tim, then he smiled. Heh
Pat mind that idea you had about saving the empties
and bashing them down, taking them to a scrappie?

Aye.

It was a fucking mad idea! Tim guffawed.

I nodded. I stared at the fire a few moments. It did
need replenishing. There was a kids' cot someplace,
some fucking thing, I couldnay remember. Tim was
saying to Arthur about the story, finish the story. I
thought he had finished it. It was a dream, I said, it wasnay a story.

Tell us it anyway, said Tim.

Aye, I said, we're all ears.

Arthur squinted at me.

Tell us, said Tim.

Ach naw, a stupid dream.

Stupidity hasnay stopped ye before, I said.

Thanks Pat.

Nicky Parkes glanced at me then at Arthur.

I was gony go for the burnables then I thought Naw, I
want to hear the cunt. Get it ower and done with, I said.

Arthur sniffed and continued, repeating some of the
earlier stuff for the benefit of Nicky Parkes. I only half
listened. I hadnay heard much the first time and what I

was hearing now didnt greatly interest me. I find that stuff childish, like dirty jokes and that kind of shite, boring crap.

The beer was tasty, given the label was foreign and I could not remember having seen it before. Some of it trickled down my chin. I wiped it with the cuff of my coat sleeve.

Parties were watching me. I'll wring it out later, I said, once yous mob have fucked off.

Charming, said Tim.

You dont have to listen, said Arthur.

I sighed. Know something Arthur you are a shifty cunt.

No as shifty as you man you're a byword in this parish.

Parish, oho, the Pape patter. This is mixed company you behave yerself.

Finish the story, said Tim.

Arthur shrugged. I'm no inventing fuck all

It's a dream, said Tim.

Exactly. I knew the two guys, Arthur said, but it wasnay like we were pals. It's more like we used to be pals. Years ago. We had went our separate ways and just bumped into each other.

So what ye saying?

Well it's obvious. The two of them were shagging the same bird.

What do ye mean 'obvious'?

The way things happen in a dream, said Arthur. Ye just know. He was a nasty fucker. He was pointing back down the lane. I looked to see what he was pointing at.

Sure enough it was the other guy, his mate, the first yin's mate. I watches the two of them laughing and joking the gether.

Aw jees, I said, I'm lost.

That is how I felt, said Arthur, fucking sidelined man. I thought These three bastards are keeping me out of it.

Ye mean you wanted yer hole as well?

Tim laughed.

Naw Pat I dont mean that.

Well what then?

It was like They know something I dont.

Tim stopped laughing and said, Who was the woman?

Arthur nodded. I was wondering when somebody would ask that.

Nicky Parkes sniffed, cleared his throat and cleared his tubes, dumped the lot on the fire.

I hope it's no about us, I said. I hate stories about where that happens, where a guy winds up his wife's having it away with some cunt. It's as auld as the hills and it will never stop but that doesnay mean ye've got to like hearing about it. Personally speaking I dont like hearing about it, no if it is mates involved.

Nicky Parkes looked at me, then at Tim, then swigged from his can, wiped his mouth.

Ye want to hear my dreams, I said, they're fucking murder fucking polis man. Mind you I dont usually get any. And see if I do, they're fucking boring as fuck. No kidding ye man they're that fucking boring I dont remember having them once they've gone. Nay fucking wonder!

Nicky Parkes spluttered. He spluttered and sput-
tered. He went into a fit. It started with a giggle. Then
the beer went up or down his gullet, nose and tubes. He
definitely had something wrong in the nostrils department. I slapped him on the back. When he was able to
speak he said, Sorry man ye just made me laugh there.

I'm glad of that, I said, I like making cunts laugh.

Tim said, Tell ye my problem, I cannay get to sleep.

If yer dreams were really boring then they would
make ye go to sleep.

Arthur wagged his finger at me. Pat, he said, ye
wouldnay get dreams if ye were awake. Ye would be
already sleeping.

What is this April fool! I said. What day is it?

What about the third man? said Tim, I want to know
about him. The one the two guys met.

It was me they met, said Arthur, I was the third man.

So it was your wife? said Tim.

What?

Is that the punchline?

There's nay punchline.

Nicky Parkes leaned closer to me and said quietly,
What did he say there?

I shrugged.

The dream just went on, said Arthur, the two guys
were taking me down the lane.

What were they wanting to shag you as well?

Pat gie us a break?

Well nay wonder, I said, fucking *Gone with the Wind*. I
swigged another mouthful, wiped my chin with my

coat sleeve. I didnay like the way this was going but could do nothing to stop it, bar go for the burnables. But it wouldnay stop the dream being telled, just me from hearing it. And if these cunts heard it I needed to.

At the same time I wasnay wanting to be dishonest. Arthur had persisted in telling us it. Maybe I was doing him a disservice. Okay he was a shifty cunt but he wasnay an arsehole. And now he was looking at me. What ye looking at me for?

What?

I stared at him.

I'm just telling the story.

Well tell the fucking story.

Okay. So the lassie comes out the house and she looks about. There's a wee flight of stairs. It's like she is looking for the next guy along. She doesnay see us, me and the other two guys, she just doesnay see us. The funny thing is I recognize her. She's wearing a blue and black speckled jersey and a black skirt and she's got a jacket on, a kind of blazer type of thing, and she's wearing black tights.

Black tights! said Tim. I might have known.

Me and all, said Nicky Parkes, and his eyebrows twitched.

We need burnables, I said, I know where there's cardboard boxes.

Want a hand? said Tim.

Naw.

Get a bottle of wine while ye're at it, said Nicky Parkes.

Ha ha, I said but away I went.

Vacuum

She was moving around. She would be tidying. She did
this to keep up her spirits. Thump thump. No she did
not, she did it to make me feel guilty. One thing was for
sure, there was no need to tidy. Nobody ever visited the
place. How come she had to tidy? How come she kept
on tidying? Morning noon and night it drove me crazy.
The girls never visited, nobody visited. The last people
to visit were neighbours with a burst pipe who shouted
about water coming through their ceiling. It had not
come through any ceiling, it came down through the
light. The water followed the track of the wire: electri-
cal wire. They failed to notice. Stupidity. They were
lucky they had not short-circuited the entire block of
flats. That was a month ago. The wife did the talking,
she was good at that kind of stuff. I could not look at
them. Except for the postman that was the last visitors.
We had sons. They never came. When was the last
time? I could not remember. A month ago at least. Of
course they had their own lives. Of course.

This tidying and dish washing drove me up the wall;
counter cleaning, washing machines, mopping the linoleum, polishing the bloody ornaments and hoovers
hoovers hoovers. What a din! That is what it was, a pan-
demonium, if you were trying to read so you needed to

concentrate. I tried to concentrate. It was not easy. Nothing was easy. Not nowadays either; it was hard reading at all without her to contend with. I determined to ignore it, including the sound of her moving, she would move, move, move move move, to irritate me. She done it to irritate me. She said it was to make me aware of reality. That was the way she put it, as though reality had given me the slip. She could get on with life roundabout, the daily grind, unlike myself; this is what she meant.

Oh, I said, okay, right, of course, you're so much more at home in the world than I am. Excuse me. It is so obviously the case why bother talking about it. So obvious I forgot.

No answer.

The door was ajar. I pushed it further open, enough to shout through: What exactly is this reality you keeping talking about? Just tell me, I would be very interested to hear.

No answer.

Eh! I said. Do you know something the rest of us dont?

Still no answer. She knew a trap when she heard it; I would have something up my sleeve. If she replied she would be finished. I would get her. I would have something lined up to say, and I would say it. She was cornered. She was. I had her. She knew it now, if not already, I mean before, I think she would have, definitely.

But it wearied me. I retreated to the kitchen, shut the door, sat down at the table. I closed my eyes. I opened them. It was true: I was trying to get her cornered. That is what I was doing. Looking for ways to attack. It was quite bad, even perhaps despicable, if you were describing it.

It was our lives. This is what it had come to. And it was me responsible. She was not doing it. It was me. I was doing it.

I needed to straighten myself out. It was not her it was me.

But I was at a low ebb. I knew it. She did too. Both of us. It applied to our relationship as a whole. Although it was me especially. I accept that. I would never have denied it. There was something up with me and I could not get myself out of it. I tried but could not. I needed to and I wanted to, if only I could and I would, if she would help, if only she would, and she could. She had it in her power.

Oh but she had such faith in my mental strength! So she said. Not in so many words. It was all unspoken with her.

My mental strength. Some hopes. My mental strength had gone. Did I have any to begin with? She thought I did. She thought I could sort out myself, like how I sorted out everything else.

She was being sarcastic.

But I could have, and I would have. Of course I would have. As long as I knew what it was. Then I would deal with it. You have to know the situation. She spoke about reality but that was reality. If you were unaware of the situation then you could not deal with it. She could have

helped but she did not. Even to let me think, if she had
let me think, let me think and I would work it out. She
did not let me think. All this tidying and cleaning nonsense. How could a body think! Washing and bloody polishing. It should have been reminders she was giving me,
not all this racket racket racket damn racket. That was a
pure attack. It was help I needed and she attacked me.

I needed help, to handle the situation. It was not only
for my sake. It was the two of us. We would both suffer. Did she want us to suffer? Maybe she did, she hated
me that much. Else why attack the person closest to
you? This is what she was doing. Why would you attack
the person closest to you? It is a contradiction. Maybe I
was not the person closest to her at all; maybe it was
somebody else. At our age! Why not? Why not at our
age? In this world anything is possible. People and
things we regard as immovable, they are not; things
change and so do people; your soul mate turns out to
be something else.

But I knew that was not how it was, I knew it was
not, it was only how she did things and got it into her
head, if she would just not get things in her head.

There was no sound now.

Of course not. She had been at it all morning and
needed a rest, she would want a cup of tea, and could
not get one. She could not get one because I was here,
in the kitchen, so she could not come in and put on a
kettle of water. What a situation. I got up from the
table and opened the door, went ben the front room.
The hoover was there but she was not.

She was in the bedroom, sitting on the bed. She looked up, surprised to see me. I smiled. Why attack me? I said. I'm the person closest to you in this whole rotten world.

I dont think it's a rotten world.

Well I do.

I dont.

My world's rotten.

Well dont drag me into it, she said. She did not look at me when she spoke. I preferred her to look. I was looking at her. She knew I was. Just dont drag me into it, she said.

I'm not going to.

Then dont.

I waited a moment. Now she glanced at me. I knew she would. I just knew she would. I dont want to drag you into anything, I said, and I wish I didnt have to.

Well you dont have to, she said. You dont have to at all. You dont. Go away and drag somebody else. Why are you smiling?

Who me?

Why are you smiling?

I'm not smiling, I said, except at this point I did smile. It was unfair and I knew it was unfair. Blatantly unfair. Yet still I did it. Sometimes I have a thing in me; I know that I am a man. We both do. She is weaker, as a woman. It is just a physical thing. I have the physical strength. I have it in me. She is so much weaker. I could just hit her. I could. I would not like to say what I could do to her. She was staring at me. She did not know what I was

229

thinking. It was inside my head. She did not know what went on. I was glad she did not. I needed her not to. People need their space and their privacy, me too. Sometimes she looked at me. I did not like how she did it.

But it was my fault. It was. I knew it was. If she would just help me, why did she not? I wished she would. I honestly did. But she did not even talk, she did not talk, why did she not talk it drove me actual mad, just straight angry mad that was what she did and she did not have to, she just did it. Did she even know I had her cornered? Of course she did but what did she do about it? Nothing. I wanted to scream. She reached for a pillow; why I do not know. I do not know why. What was a pillow going to do, a piece of flimsy cotton or wool or some stuff. She did not speak. Why did she not speak? That aggravated me. She did aggravate me, she had it in her power and she used that power. She had her power. Women do. She did.

She was looking at me but then was not, just at the carpet floor; if she needed to hoover, maybe she was wondering.

She knew how this would start. The very words that came out my mouth. It did not depress me. Her challenge on reality was the key. I had not replied openly. I pretended to mishear. We might have been watching television for all the difference it would have made. I brought it up out the blue and her heart sank. I was smiling. I was unable to stop myself. Even before saying it I was smiling. At the very idea! She would have been expecting it but not even knowing she was expecting it!

Until I did it. Then she would. And she was beat. She knew she was beat. She knew I had beat her, just cornered, she was cornered.

How had I managed it? It was so good I felt like writing it down for future situations. It was a beauty. I could have written it down on an old envelope if I had found one, also a pen, if I could find one of them. But we did not keep them in the bedroom. Bedrooms were not there for that purpose. Envelopes and pens were for the front-room writing-cabinet just like cups and saucers were for the kitchen and vacuum cleaners the walk-in lobby cupboard.

I had no interest in any of that. The present was difficult enough. Just concentration concentration, that was the key, apply the brains, the grey matter. Or so I thought. Only for a moment or two. Who was kidding who?

But what was it? I wondered. Even the way she was looking at me. How come she was looking at me? I looked at her. I stared at her. It was not hard to do.

*Pieces of shit do not have
the power to speak.*

Date of arrival: April.

Another dream laid waste.

I had prepared my defence but when the time came they gave me no chance to deliver it. I wasnt allowed to shave and my hair was in an unkempt condition. The Accompanying Officer showed me into court, told me where to stand and the proper way of standing. The Court Official read out the bare facts of the charges so rapidly I had little time to mumble your Honour, Lordship or Worship and wondered what term I was supposed to use hereabouts. Different authorities different formalities. The Court Official's speech consisted of rambling passages that degenerated into confused utterings. Then he added a bit on. I was to be kept in the cell for seven more days, then taken to the port of departure, set on to a boat and returned posthaste to the mainland. A clerk coughed. From local-government coffers a sum was to be settled with the shipping company such that a single fare might be purchased.

I smiled, a reflex action which only antagonized the Accompanying Officer. The fellow gripped my wrist forcibly once they departed the inner area. I allowed it. What else could I have done. I smiled again. I was going to speak, I said, I thought I would have had the chance to speak.

Didnt nobody tell you you're a piece of shit, pieces of shit dont speak.

I nodded. It sounded sensible.

I had to hold onto my jeans at the waistband, they had taken my belt and my belly had shrunk. Skin and bone. When I lay on my back the skin at the front rested on the skin at the back. The cell entrance was ahead. Now. And I flexed my upper arm in preparation for the push in the back. When it came I went: Aaahhh! to improve the Officer's temper. Useless being a right-wing sadist bastard if naybody notices. He was a heavy lump of a man and could have knocked the stuffing out me. If he had caught me. What they call a big clumsy ox. I was wiry and slippery and could escape from tight corners. I also packed a punch. The Officer maybe inferred as much and gave me a lengthy stare. Just you try it buddy. Such was the guy's thought. Yet Accompanying Officers are also human beings. The doors closed solidly, with a juicy kind of thump.

I stepped back and sat on the edge of the palliasse. Here was reality and yes it was grim. A time for reflection, when fellow beings are excused scrutiny.

Later I felt better.

Too soon for a wank. It was to be used for sedation purposes only. Okay. I pondered the past days. My sorry luck; it had been so bad there was nothing to be done, nothing to be said. Bemoan it, then proceed. Life would continue even though I had been absented from it. But

Pieces of shit do not have the power to speak.

if this palliasse had been available to me a few days ago then I would have been okay. I patted it. You should have been mine, I said, I would've taken care of you, kept you warm in winter.

So I was talking to a bed, so what.

Yet a sigh was warranted. This was to have been paradise. The only thing better than not working was not working in a land of sunny climes. This was such a land, where young women tourists freely gave of themselves to local young males of unmanacled spirit, suntanned and with healthy limbs.

Why do suntans and healthy limbs enter it? The unmanacled spirit one can understand. Outdoor lives! I was thinking of those, where one could become fit and well, a lithe individual; maybe working as a beachguard. Once upon a time I could swim. If I escaped from the island gaol then certainly I might throw myself into the sea and thresh towards the horizon.

But really, I didnay want to be deported. Had the Court Official stated such categorically? Perhaps he meant something else. Ambiguity was a feature in small southern towns. Sure they had found me 'lurking' beside the garbage bins down a 'back alley'. But all alleys are out the back and anyone found in such a byway is said to be 'lurking'. Come on now tell the truth and state the case fairly: Mr Duncan was sheltering from a gale wind.

I was. That was a hellish gale wind and no mistake. Sure I had the smell of alcohol on my breath. What in God's teeth was wrong with that? I was twenty-one years of age and beyond the age of legitimacy. It was my first day in the place and I had got ashore safely, safely. A celebration had been in order. Such behaviour was normal. What did 'normality' mean in this here burg.

No job; okay. Abode there was none; okay. Cash ditto; nothing new in that. And no Verifiable Information as to Previous Whereabouts. So they said. Mr Duncan begged to differ. I did. I offered to verify anything, anything. To no avail. Then too, there also existed, and freely confessed: Bad Tidings from a certain Ship's Restaurant.

Such was the crime, such the criminal.

At 4.30 a.m. they had chanced upon me. My first day in the place. Two glaring flashlights inches from my eyes. Eighteen hours earlier could life have been rosier! Bestriding the upper decks in jaunty fashion bidding fellow passengers G'day.

Envious stares all round. I had been the only person left at the bar with a pint of stout in front of me. That was no sentimental nonsense. Truly the case. A six-hour sail had become a ten-hour battle through some of the worst seas the stewards had witnessed in fifteen years on the run. So they said.

Ah but it suited me. I was trying a new approach to life and so far it was working. It was simple. I had ceased being stand-offish. I was always interested in the lives of other people but in the past had looked on from afar. The idea of opening a conversation with a guy behind the bar would have been unthinkable, even more unthinkable that I would carry it forwards. But I persisted and

the barman repaid me by blethering on about all manner
of oddities, some boring, some not so boring.

At long last I was becoming a sociable animal. It was
bound to aid my job prospects. I bought the guy a couple of black rums, then tried one myself. I sniffed at it
firstly. Mm, an okay aroma. But the taste itself made
me groo. The barman was relishing his. Black rum was
a tradition, a fighting tradition. Besides being an old
salt he was a decent guy and chatted away about life in
general. He came from a wee island himself and had
been raised to a life of easy servitude. He was even
content! Tips were good and although a married man
of somewhat advanced years, female tourists beckoned
occasionally.

It sounded the thing to me. But were there vacancies
aboard the boat? I was set to enquire but for some
reason the thought of work vanished from my mind. I
certainly fancied life as a sailor. On short trips definitely.
But if pushed I would hire on for longer sojourns. On
ocean-going vessels only. Above all they must be sea-
worthy!

These ruminations were at an end when came an
announcement. Last orders for the restaurant which
soon would be closing.

But man man man I was starving! I had not noticed
this until that very moment! This call to knives and
forks had been announced for me and me only. There
was naybody else left. I bade the barman G'day and
followed my nose to midships. I had to hold on to ban-
isters and walls. The sea was going up and down to

heights my fellow travellers found tricky and the floors were slippery with a mixture of vomit and the golden briny. But the God of Empty Bellies urged me on. Shipahoy, I was starving.

The place was empty. A waiter showed me to a table and passed me a sheaf of menu pages. I thanked him, nodded appreciatively at the listed contents then ordered a meal that would plunder more than half of my entire life savings. But Gahd sir it was worth every coin. A three-course meal, plus a half carafe of casa rosa. The Starter I had was this: the **Chef Special with Prawns and Mussels and Choice Fruits à la Mer** and it came in a fishblood gravy – how else to describe it – with wee splashes of syrup at the side of the plate and a skinny trail of green peppery stuff. And thick bread to wipe it up; a sweet bread with a cake-like crust that one hesitates to describe as crust at all and yet as tasty a bread as ever succumbed to my advances.

I was not alone after all. Gadzooks. This reached the higher slopes of sentimentality. Two fine-looking elderly ladies were to the side of the room, having a laugh together, both tucking into whatever it was, marzipan jelly and devilled ice cream with marshmallow sauce, chocolate nuts and very thin, mint biscuits, onchontay madames. These ladies were French, a la chic chic

Meanwhile strong men crumbled, their bellies succumbing to the heaving seas. Why oh why did we have the last six pints of stout, they screamed to an uncaring hurricane! Or was it eight pints? Oh for fuck sake, Quick quick quick, was the shout, and which way doth the wild wind blow? Always spew portside. Such I had learned from a venerable sage of the sea.

Between courses I endured a moment's anxiety. Okay now my life had been short. Who could argue with that? Me! I would have argued. It had been forever! But I had already ordered the grub so no way back. Sink or swim.

For the main dish I ordered another **Chef Special**. And never antagonize a Chef. We all know that. Chefs are unpredictable creatures in diverse ways when off-duty but not in the fucking kitchen.

But no Chef worth his salt ever disliked a trencher-man. Any Chef worth his weight in biscuits was above and beyond the call of La cuenta por favor. For any creature such that that creature was a Chef, what occurred on the plate was the sole and overriding issue.

The strict course of action was to finish the plate and wipe it clean, to cry for bread and sook up the gravy. That gave one a head start. Sympathy would be mine. Whereas to order such a meal and dilly-dally with it! A veritable slap on the face. No Chef worthy of the name could endure the insult.

It was true. I knew it for a fact. I had experience of Chefs, having worked in a restaurant on three occasions, howsomever in a cleansing capacity, having failed to traverse the higher rungs of the cookery ladder.

For the Main Course, oh boy: **Halibut Steak in Basic Garlic Sauce, with Chargrilled Tomatoes and Okra**. Chargrilled tomatoes! A girl of a loquacious bent once advised me that along the Chargrilled vegetable route lay a cancerous labyrinth, that once entered could only advance. What did I care. Plus a mélange of thick red onions, red cobweb cabbage and chunky red peppers. Placed alongside this a pewter bowl with a further trio of vegetables: dark-green broccoli, blue-white cauliflower and slender green items that may have been beansprouts, peapods, or a luxury vegetable item rarely seen on workaday dinner plates and whose name seldom registers in the brain of such as oneself, to wit, me. Little wonder the two elderly ladies laughed so loudly. I waved across.

A waiter lingered by the ladies' table for a moment's conversation, poured tea from the pot. I noticed that the fellow's crisp white teacloth dragged from his elbow across the dessert plates. It must have been the roll of the sea for these waiters were top-notch servers, given they operated as gigolos on the side and were wont to exhibit a smug exhaustion. Of course I envied them. Of course I did. I was a personable young fellow. The position of gigolo was not beyond me.

Ah but a most delicious and succulent repast. The waiter now served me **Choice Cuts of Cheese and Rare Stuffed Olives**. One's compliments to the Chef. A brandy to follow would have been injudicious. On second thoughts

No. No second thoughts. Not even the cheese and Stuffed Olives. I moved to a leather seat by a porthole. The shutter had been drawn. I tried to push it up but it was set fast. It would have been too narrow to clamber through. I knew how to clamber through narrow apertures but this would have been impossible, certainly in consideration of the recent repast.

And alack alack alack oh, the waiter was presenting a la cuenta. He was of a kindly demeanour. I smiled and accepted the slip of paper. I folded it twice over without looking, slipping it into my pocket. I toyed with it for many minutes, unable to confront what could only be a disaster. Life had never been easy. Today was no different. I glanced sideways and roundabout.

And the porthole cover remained stationary. By a glazed display cabinet the waiter was reading a folded newspaper. By the upper-deck exit stood his uniformed colleague. I was on guard misooh!

Ach well.

Time certainly passed. Where had the elderly women gone?

I was in a state of extreme dolority, always a time for sore reflection. But what transpired during this time for sore reflection is anyone's guess. Did I faint? I was resting with my head against the side of the wall, on the other side of which raged a hostile sea. Maybe I dozed. I sighed and my breast heaved and my heart was heavy, and oh, all manner of self-castigatory musings were mine. My fuck. I couldnt afford the damn meal what in God's teeth was I to do may the decks open up and the seven seas swallow me oh Lord, for such would have been my fervent prayer had I been inclined towards such a course. Oh Maid de la Mer rescue me.

But no such rescue occurred. Reality had never been more stark. At last the light tap on the shoulder. I sighed and braced myself. It was more of a bad dream than a nightmare.

Both waiters were before me: We are approaching the harbour sir. The doors of this restaurant are closing, they are closed.

I have no money.

You cannot settle the bill sir?

I cannot, no.

They sighed.

I apologize, truthfully. I do not have the money. I over-extended myself. Is there a Catering Manager?

You have no credit card sir?

No.

It must go badly for you.

Is there nothing can be done? Your food was just so good and enticing I mean it was just so so good.

The waiters shook their head. It was apparent that what was happening had not been unforeseen. They had spotted me from the outset. They knew me for a risk. Och well. All to the good. Such was my conclusion.

I shrugged but my brains were going nineteen to the dozen as my grannie used to say. Where was my grannie now, now that I needed that venerable worthy? She would have gathered me unto her vast skirts and hidden me asunder.

The harbour police greet our arrival, said one waiter.

You will be handed over to them, said the other.

May I go to the upper deck until then?

Alas no, it is not permitted.

Pieces of shit do not have the power to speak.

I nodded. Nothing was to be done. Once more I was afoul of the Fates. I closed my eyes and imagined stepping over bodies to the upper deck and outside, letting the wind blow the sweaty staleness from my clothes, the rain like buckshot, one's head bowed, the scalp spattered.

I again prayed. In an earlier time I prayed regularly to ward off evil and to bring material gain. How come I gave it up? Goodness me.

The storm abated. The small islands would have emerged from the heavy mist and torrential rain.

Soon the ship docked, the passengers disembarked; the two elderly ladies, the dishevelled and recovering stout drinkers, the lithe-legged female tourists.

I alone, I alone.

The waiters sat by the upper-deck exit. This left the lower-deck exit. I might make my way below, a speedy search for lost coins, lost bags and other properties. But this would be futile.

Life was beyond me. It had never been sweet. Adequate luck was all I sought; the occasional discarded, half-eaten jellied pork pie. But ah me, the stuff of dreams. I saw the waiters. One dozed. Had I tried a fly move they would have been instantly alert. Instead I called: Hullo!

They looked across.

I have discovered money! May I now settle the bill in full?

Yes, they said.

The difficulty is that it represents three quarters of my entire life savings.

Ours also sir, we are a poor people.

On a previous occasion and in a different location I had landed in a new town at the start of a new life with funds whose extension was negated by one coffee and a cheese and pickle sandwich. I thought to narrate this to the waiters. They would have been interested.

Nothing was to be done. My pockets were not vast. I brought forth the money and concluded the transaction. The waiters nodded me towards the exit.

Lubbers yawned as I stepped down the gangway. Apart from the boatstaff I was last man ashore.

I strolled the nearby streets and alleyways, familiarizing myself with the landmarks. Evening approached. I returned to the promenade and a small coffee stall, but it had closed. I moved to a pub and eavesdropped conversations, sipped long on water, hoping for reports on temporary abodes and immediate job prospects.

Then it was closing time. The barman was upturning chairs on to the tops of tables. The pub doors were open. I had to leave. My bag was at my feet. I lifted it and walked.

Later I settled myself on a bench, and tried to doze. But a hurricane appeared as from nowhere. I returned to the nearby streets and alleyways, seeking a likely place, a place of repose. Enter Officers with Flashlights.

Tomorrow the sun would shine, cooking the tar on the roads, upon which feet might squelch. On the walk to the beach an agreeable suffering. Of course posing along the hot sands, flicking grains of sand onto people's skin, stepping across brown curvy bodies, whither a one

Pieces of shit do not have the power to speak.

may rise and follow, an heiress searching for the simple unmanacled life, the sensual masculine animal to lead her and show her that which exists for the bolder imaginations, and how to take it without disturbing other souls, to spend that fortune wisely, seeking only happiness at a cost other than rippling waves, and so on, into the water. Enter Officers with Flashlights.

Ach well.

One day I would gaze back upon this escapade wistfully. Yes me hearties, this yere were the point my whole life did change.

I sipped at the mug of water. A uniformed fellow had brought me this mug of water. The Gaoler. He looked ages with me and was self-conscious, almost embarrassed. In another life we might have gone to the same school or else been a pair of coconuts on the same tree, if one believed in reincarnation. Some of these beliefs embraced the world of objects; former or future lives might include lower vegetative states. Fanciful but appealing. Coconuts too have a life. They hang beneath a clear sunny sky, sipping their own palm wine, gazing upon a placid sea.

The sex life of coconuts.

My ferry fare back to the effing mainland had been paid by the island authorities. I would have accepted half of that sum roundly and in the palm of my hand. It would have enabled me to go forth on a full stomach to seek work and sustenance. I would have accomplished the mission. Never no more would I have been a burden on the island citizenry.

Honest!

In the name of God's teeth it was surely bad socio-logical economics to deport me to the effing mainland. In days past such offers were surely afforded the more exotic beggar. And I was of that ilk.

Date of departure: April.

I aimed a kick at the palliasse but did not perform the action. Instead I flopped into the corner that had become my favourite. I once considered joining the regular army as an escape from reality. Now here I was.

Why had the Accompanying Officer not allowed me to shave and get my hair in order?

I belonged to that class of fellow whose existence antagonized a particular kind of older male. The Court had been composed of these Older Males. A 'smart appearance' was always of the essence. Thus had the Court Official stared upon me, lips curling, nostrils flaring. He coughed three times before speaking, which denoted a grave conclusion:

Pieces of shit do not have the power to speak.

All aboard!

These and similar musings. I lay on a palliasse in a cell six feet long by six feet wide, or was this too a part of the dream? Would I awaken from this?

In the outside world people enjoyed living. The sun shone. The salty island air, the salty freshwater.

In the town dungeon, a young man of sound limb awaits a ship to points north.

Points north. I stopped talking, for I had been talking, not to an imaginary listener but to myself, hands

Pieces of shit do not have the power to speak.

clasped behind my head. Not a time for reflection. That too had passed.

The grey ceiling. Trails across it. These trails were silvery. Snails climb walls and cross ceilings. A snail with sturdy suction soles. The world be its oyster. No dungeons in snailworld.

justice for one

They were marching already when I fought my way to the meeting point up the hill. Now there were voices all around, and of every kind. I was blundering about not understanding what I was to do. How did they know and I did not?

Somebody tried to sell me something or give me something I was unsure which. Somebody else asked me a question. I was not sure about that either. I could not decipher what they wanted to know or even understand what they said. Was it even myself they were talking to? I heard someone saying: Shit he's drunk out his skull.

Me? I was not drunk, not drunk out my skull. Shit man I was not drunk at all. What the hell were they on about? I asked them but they paid no attention. They had made up their mind.

This is what people do, especially in this part of the world. A woman said, We're going this way.

What way? I said but the woman had gone, whoever she was.

A typical life experience. Women go away: it could be the title of a Spanish movie. Probably it is already.

On all sides folk were walking past. They moved quickly. Some were coming so close I felt a draught from their body, going to bang into me. Somebody said, The army are there and they are waiting for us.

I shouted, I beg your pardon!

Take your hand off my arm, cried a man.

Sorry mate, it is so damn dark and all that smelling smelly shit; what is that smell? said another man, somebody with a hoarse voice. He had quite a kindly voice, and he added, Better get out of here … And then he grasped my wrist.

Hey, I said, dont do that. Whereabouts are they anyway?

Down the hill.

Are there many?

I dont know friend, somebody said there were hundreds.

For God sake!

I know. And coming in our direction! Then the hoarse man smiled. He actually smiled.

Did you say our direction? I said.

He only smiled at me. He was no longer holding my wrist, and I had that sense he was about to vanish from in front of my eyes. I wanted to keep him here, just like hold him back, not let him escape, he was escaping. How come I couldnt escape but he can! That was me, that is what I was thinking. Jesus, our direction, how come?

Instead of answering he glanced at another marcher, another woman; this one had a band wrapped round her forehead and some hair falling over its sides; her cheeks were smudged and the blood was there. He jerked his thumb in my direction, shaking his head in a

gesture to her, about me, as if I was somebody to avoid.
But I was only wanting to know why they were marching from that direction. I shouted: How come? Surely
that's the question.

What do you mean? muttered the woman. I dont like
the way you are saying that.

But if they're marching from that direction! I said.
Then I stopped and shrugged. She did not care.

I could see another couple of people looking at me;
they too were suspicious. I shook my head at them, as
if I was just seeing them for the first time.

It was dreadful. But what could I do except walk on.
This is what I did, yes, I kept walking. Of course I did.
So that was it. Much was explained, even to predictabi-
lity. One of the folk watching stopped directly in front
of me. Another woman. There were many women, yet
I could not pass her without making a nonsensical comment. I stopped walking to do it. The earth is good.
I said it into myself though perhaps my lips moved.
I wondered about myself. It was a surprise I had any
self-respect at all. I asked the woman what was wrong,
if something was wrong and she replied. You will not
get far.

Sure I will.

Not the way we're going. She put her hands onto my
wrists and tugged me forwards.

What the hell are you doing? I said.

She smiled. My attention was attracted to her shoulders. It was not a time for physical attraction. Her
shoulders were beautiful. At the point where the

machine gun opens up on you, on you, your attention is drawn to the curve of a woman, a woman's shoulders. My God, almost I was crying.

Saddened by something. I saw it in her. This was a thought she had had, and in connection with myself. But not sex, it could never have been sex, to have been with me, lying with me, it could never have been that. Shit man. No. Never. She was pointing in the same direction the crowd had marched. Okay. That is the way ahead, she said, that is a proper march.

Yes but that is also how the crowd is advancing. Do you wish me to follow the crowd. Is that an elitist thing to say?

She was gazing at me.

Do you think it is?

She thought I was mad. You do, I said, I can see you do. It is a terribly elitist thing to say.

Now she avoided eye-contact. Just keep walking straight, she said, and stay to the rear.

I shall miss the action.

Is that not what you want? The difference is you will not go wrong.

Oh.

Yes.

So that is the difference?

Yes.

I said, But how do you know what I want?

But I looked at her shoulders when I said it, and I did that so she would notice. It was almost disgusting. I think it was disgusting.

She shook her head. Perhaps she was ashamed of me.

I smiled. You think you know me but you dont. You dont even know when I am being sarcastic.

She turned her back to me, and resumed walking. I managed not to go after her, nor to call after her. There are times for being funny, this was not one of them. I saw a man spit on the road. It was in regard to me! He was spitting against me!

Shit. What had I done to deserve that. Talking to the woman with the beautiful shoulders. Perhaps he thought it demeaning, that it demeaned us all. He also walked away. Then the chanting began:

Justice for one justice for all.

I looked for the woman but she too had gone.

So many people, they just started chanting, and these slogans. There was nothing wrong with these slogans. I tried to say the words aloud and succeeded. I was pleased. I said the words again. I was laughing, just how I could say them, just as good as anyone.

We all were marching. Armed forces march and so do people. We marched over the brow of the hill. I knew the terrain.

I listened to the slogans and knew them as fair. These were good words, except the way I said them they sounded different, they sounded as though different, as if in some way singular, they became words to actually decipher, as opposed to a slogan, the sort that one marches to. I tried to pick up that latter rhythm, the way everyone else had it. Justice for one justice for all. Great rhythms, great slogans but could I do it? Or was

I only emulating the passion of these other people? As a boy I missed the beat – I always missed the beat. Now here it was again, half a line behind, I was half a line behind, behind everyone else.

Justice for one justice for all. Nothing wrong in that. I walked briskly on, one foot in front of the other. A peculiar sensation overtook me. I could no longer see things clearly. People and objects blurred, was that a building or was it a jumbo aircraft? Where the hell was I was this a city street or was it a country lane? was that a herd of animals or what, what was it? Over now some yards distant somebody was – her, it was her again, it was that woman, one of the women, it was one of the women, which one was she? She was watching me. Hey! I waved to her but she ignored the wave; she was still watching me, and then not.

Beyond here were things. And what things! Things that were guaranteed to scare me. Some folk were heroes. This woman was one of them. Obviously she was. And the man who seemed her companion. I saw him too. Both were heroes. It could not be denied. Their actions were heroic. Mine were not. The very idea! I smiled. Beyond the current conglomeration I could not perceive one entity, not one single entity, not one, not that.

It was where they were walking, it was down a hill, it is where they were going. And everybody shouting different things, slogans and laughter, somebody, trying to start a new chant, people were. And now the army were into view. Everybody knew it, there was a shiver now and some folk threw down cigarettes and trampled them and others again opened their packets and got out another and snatched at them with their lighters.

If it was for men was it for women! I asked the first person next to me, a middle-aged woman in her forties or maybe fifties.

I beg your pardon?

Is it for men, or is is it meant to be women as well? I'm not keen on women being here.

I dont know what you are talking about.

But what does it all mean? I said. I never ever work it out, I was never able to.

What did you say? The woman seemed irritated.

Dont take it too seriously, I said.

A couple of younger fellows rushed past now, arms laden with stones. That meant the army right enough, there would be a pitched battle. That was how it went. History showed us this. It did not require demonstration upon demonstration and does not entail actual changes in how we live our life. I had to go with them, I shouted and ran ahead.

I am as Putty

Things had been desperate for the last couple of days but I had to be at the Agency for 11 o'clock. The usual crackdown. That is what they call it, officialdom. Fucking officialdom man I hate it, I detest it with a vehemence, total vehemence. And I had to prepare. It is up to you how you approach the whole thing but if you dont try you dont succeed. A good thing was the woman that worked there. She had her own little place. An office I think, quite comfy as I recall, a desk and chairs, and just so warm, maybe too warm. You felt like telling her to turn down the heating system. But in a lot of these quasi-government places the heating gets controlled by a central body and you dont have any power to turn it down because they keep the fucking temperature the same all over.

These bureaucrats man they would do it everywhere if they could get away with it. Imagine they ruled the world, you would get the same temperature in Greenland as the Mali desert.

She was a bureaucrat too, the woman that worked there. No point denying it.

At 9 o'clock I entered the mall and into a large department store. I was starving but the choice was mine.

It was dead quiet. Monday morning I suppose. In the gents' outfitter section I squandered the remaining cash on an individual underwear pack comprising socks, boxers and tee-shirt. Preparation requires that. In the mensroom they had paper towels: excellent; that is what I hoped. Nobody was around so off came the shirt for a wash; I soaped and rinsed the armpits, doused the head with warm water, had a shave. Then to hell with it, whipped off the socks and washed my feet in the basin, squeezing the soap through the old toes, oh man, such fucking heavenly bliss man what a sensation, what a truly amazing sensation. One felt like a Lordship. Yes your Lordship?

One's toes, there is a good fellow.

I dried them with the paper towels which were not ideal, but so what man so what. It wouldnt be my fault if matters turned sour, were the world of work and sweat to look unfavourably upon one. Responsibility was mine!

The skin was damp when I pulled on the new socks but they felt so damn comfortable that I thought of wearing them alone. I could tie together the laces of the boots and carry them round my neck.

Ah but the trusty old socks, boo hoo, they were finished now, the time had come to bid farewell. They had been through thick and thin together them two but I had to make the hard decision. Farewell old fellows. I stuffed them behind the pipe behind the lavatory bowl. Hey! Maybe I could wash the bollocks? Now that was a thing. The washhand basin in the public area. Could

I risk it but that was the question, if somebody came in, they would think – well, I do not know what they would think. Ach, ye only live twice. No doubt they would phone the trusty old bobbies; that is what foreigners do, given it was me that was the foreigner.

The washhand basin was a bad idea if not out the question. I checked the cisterns in the cubicle. This was the place for a wash. The water from there is used to flush the bowl but is good clean water. Not clean enough for drinking except if you boil it but good enough for the genitalia. If the cistern is the right height from the floor – roughly hip height – then you can even dip them, just depending. Not today though, too risky. An intuition was strong upon me and I sensed a need: caution. Mondays are quiet but one may feel 'a presence' on such a day. Maybe it is in-store training and you are the Guinea Pig. You dont know you are, you are just a customer browsing about and doing what you do but all the time you are being surveilled, unbeknownst, a crowd of store employees are observing your every movement.

So dont tempt the luck. This is the essence of the human condition, we always fucking tempt the luck. Why not leave? There is a time to walk away. It isnt quitting it is walking away; to walk away is not to quit. It is a different thing. I was clean enough, just leave it at that

The mensroom had been a hundred per cent spotless when I entered, it was spotless when I left, even more spotless given the soapy-water spillage. Also myself; theretofore I was a soiled creature, now I was wholesomely clean, 95 per cent at least, the genitalia would have made it a hundred per cent and nobody can improve on a hundred per cent, not even God.

Some would argue that I am the property of – and thus belong to – 'my' Maker but I dont accept that He is my Maker, even if He does exist and whether or not I believe in that 'existence'. I reserve that right and regard it as inviolable.

I respect the intellectual property of others but not beyond the point of reason, and reason is the product of common humanity. Thus far and no more. I would be damned if it went further. How far do people go anyway? And what about 'damnation'? I cannot believe in 'damnation'. It is a weird idea. Where would it happen? Christians have all these 'places'. Especially Catholics. Purgatory. Imagine purgatory! All these unbaptized weans floating around. You would be dodging them all the time. It would be like a huge meteorite shattered in space and all these lumps of rock and dust flying about while you are hoofing it along the street. How the heck could you keep out its way? Not all of it. You would get hit by something, even if you crawled. At least one wee particle of rock. So maybe that was the damnation bit, if that was you for eternity having to dodge about the place avoiding bits of rubble or whatever, flying weans.

The gratuities plate was empty! It was next to the entrance cubicle. That was where mensroom attendants kept them but I hadnt seen it when I skipped through.

Empty. What do we say about that? There is nothing as empty as an empty gratuities plate.

The public are a miserly bunch of scallywags. Some might argue that people do a job and deserve a wage and shouldnt have to exist on gratuities.

Tips is another word. You have to get tipped.

The attendant fellow did his job, he deserved a pay. If you do a job you deserve a pay. That is what I think too. But if people dont get enough of a pay, if your boss doesnt pay you enough, if he is a sneaky bastard, you have got to get money somewhere. If you dont have any you die or get put in prison.

Unless somebody stole the gratuities. That is so unfair. That is one thing people should not do is thieve a guy's gratuities.

I quite fancied that job because you were out the way and had your own little cubby-hole. You could have your radio and your kettle and your microwave. That would be you. You wouldnt have to come out, you could just stay in there and not be bothered by fools and vaga-bonds. That would suit me, not having to cope with the brickbats of life. I bet you it suited a lot of guys. Although usually it was women did these jobs. Mensroom attend-ants. But it would suit a lot of women too, especially ones with abusive husbands, just getting away and being on their own. You could imagine the abusive husbands but if their wives were mensroom attendants. What sort of mischief are you getting up to! Bump, and they would get battered again. So if you were a woman you would want to stay in your cubby-hole forever, for the rest of your life and beyond, hiding away from the entire world with your knitting and your darning, just getting on with things now you have peace; and you could do your work there, whatever it was, rearing the next generation, that is what women do.

What do men do? I dont fucking know. Mind you, I would like to have been first person on that gratuities plate. Just laying the first coin. It reveals an honest bond between producer and consumer if it is possible to use that kind of language in the circumstances. Except if you have no cash. What do you do then? There is nothing you can do except leave a slip of paper to explain that you have no money and sincere apologies. I had a sandwich in my pocket.

But I was amazed at how good I looked on the way back out the door. There was a huge mirror at the exit. In some mirrors you look so good you want to steal them. That happens with me. This was such a mirror mirror on the wall. That was that shave, the best of them all, and the general clean and tidy-up. Even my feet, if I took off the socks and held up my feet man they would fucking sparkle. A bright red, but that bright red is a healthy red. Sparkly feet, that is what they looked like.

Except my toenails were of an extraordinary size and breadth. One time I was sleeping with a lady and during the night one of my big toes stabbed her on the leg. It gashed her and the wound bled. These are the kind of toenails I am talking about, real raggedy fuckers.

Maybe the woman at the job Agency would loan me her scissors. She would have scissors. Most women have scissors. They prepare for emergencies. I dont know one guy that keeps scissors except on the edge of a complicated knife. Women are different. Viva. She was a sexy-looking dame and I liked her. Maybe the same age as me. She had that English accent that once heralded doom for the rest of the world. I knew she would repent of that authoritative position and become as putty in my hands.

I will not say I was looking forward to seeing her. Women don frosty exteriors to keep you at bay. As a man you hope to break through the barrier. You quite fancy the battle but at the same time you think, Oh not again.

If you were married it would be different.

There were steps up to the entrance lobby. I could not remember them from the last time. But they must have been there, and were definitely there now. I walked up and into the lobby and along, and tapped the door into Reception firmly, but no one answered. I saw a sign that said ENTER. So I did. I was disappointed to find a different person at work behind the desk. A woman of indeterminate age, except older by a long chalk. I stated my business, that my presence had been sought by an indeterminate bureaucratic structure pertaining to officialdom. She scanned the diary entries for the morning, hitting a button below her desk in the process.

They all have these buttons, especially for use in emergencies. They think we dont know! Almost at once a door opened and my woman came out to get me, came out to get me.

I smiled. Yet I was disappointed, which was unexpected.

She was surprised to see me. Now that too was unexpected. At this point I realized I was not who she thought. She had my name and details and now here was I in person. I had emerged from the brackets. She recognized my person but not as a function of my clerical position, and I refer here to office rather than pastoral matters.

This was becoming a tricky encounter. She was studying me, not in a direct confrontational manner but I could see that my presence engulfed her. Or was it the other way about? No, how could it have been? But maybe. Bureaucrat women exercise a control on your very life spirit. You expect the dead hand from a male but when a women does it you are doubly dead. Really, that is what I believe. But it is also contradictory. You get left in that limbolular position. You want to improve, you want to do your best, you want to impress and stand up for yourself, and show that you can do it too; you can be a proper person and enter into your rightful station within society.

You do want to improve yourself. I did and would, if given the opportunity. All I needed was a chance! I think she appreciated that.

She returned behind her desk and I sat opposite. She was tapping the keyboard before having settled on the chair. My details would have appeared on the screen. The thought pleased me. I lowered my gaze modestly. But it was enough. She glanced up from the keyboard. The power of my fancy had entered her inner psyche. What a smile she gave me! Was it a smile? Yes, and I would say glorious. If smile it was then that is the word. What is that exchelsis stuff or does that only apply to celestial creatures? This woman was just really I dont know man I would say beautiful or even better than that, and a slightly peculiar thing about all this was how the smile, if smile it was, occurred at an early stage in these proceedings, or is that relating to wish-fulfilment? I had hoped to make her smile. Was she doing it of her own volition? I had to look twice, and a third time. Seeing her smile made me look over my shoulder before allowing myself the luxury of smiling back. Luxury is the wrong word because I did it in a furtive way, and furtive things are not a luxury. Luxury is out in the open. Who smiles out in the open? People who smile out in the open are the ones we should all try to be. Yet she smiled to see me, she did, she was overpowered by the vision, this wonderful-looking guy with the clean feet and the new shave. Lips and her nipples, lips and nipples, hands and satiny breasts. No wonder you shiver. I could feel her beneath me now raising herself; and me raising myself onto my elbows; her gaze upwards studying me and me smiling down at her, moving slowly man I had to relax, relax. Especially here, especially with her, here with her, and how my life had been. This was not the past.

Although there was something. Yes I liked her; but this was more than that. And from a recent occasion. It was not the first time I had been in her presence. Not at all, otherwise I would not have been anticipating actions and reactions. Yes I liked her but there was a subtlety here that demanded of acquaintance. Of acquaintance?

Was this déjà vu? No. I had been here before. When was I last here?

But I knew I had been here before.

Because I expected to see her. I had been here before and had been expecting to see her.

Now I was remembering. It was no comfort. If I thought it might have been I was wrong. Not badly wrong. It was only a thought after all. Not even a thought, more the glimmer of one.

And then the short-term memory, or memory span. Why in Heaven's name was she working in this Godforsaken den of bureaucracy? Maybe over late-night supper and a nightcap I could ask her and she could relax and explain herself. There was a place I knew, located less than two miles from the Agency; I could stretch to two cartons of soup and tea. But even her smile. What was it about her smile? that way people smile; men or women.

Because they know something. They know something you dont know. That is the fucking truth, horrific truth. That is how people smile, they are putting one over you, over on you.

Here was this woman, Clerical Officer, not to beat about the bush, and I was to have done something. I should have. What should I have done? My mind clenched in its effort to recall.

Something.

What the hell was it? Was I to have returned to this very Agency and forgotten? This struck the chord. Last Tuesday. My God. That is the horrific truth I had to face. No wonder officialdom had sought my presence. My memory had let me down again and quite badly this time, not short term but mid term. Although I was too young for Alzheimer's. As far as I know. Plus that other thing that relates to the effects of heavy intoxicants, the one with the Russian name, what the fuck do you call it – Kolnikovs or something. Probably it had to do with vitamins. I didnt eat enough fruit and vegetables. That was a simple fact of my life. An old guy I knew swore by used tea-bags; for some reason he regarded 'recycled tea-bags' as a close relative of fruit and vegetables. If you said to him, Have you had your daily apple yet? He would point at the used tea-bag and say, No, but I am going to eh ah …

He ended the sentence with a meaningful nod of the head.

But an interesting snippet arises here: a side of me that was not surprised by what had and was happening. I was not surprised. Why not? Because there was the vague expection of bad news. Me. I was expecting it. I now realized that and it explains my sense of disappointment at finding the woman in the office when at the same time it was my wildest hope.

Because she was the very woman. It was her! I had given it to her, the contract, bond or promise! I said that I would come along for a job interview and forgot all about the damn thing – life had intervened. It was she to whom I had rendered the promise, for Tuesday last.

Although I would not go so far as 'promise'. I would not call it an actual promise. I know when I promise and that was not a promise. I just said it. I shall come for the interview. That is what I told her. I did tell her that. So it was an interview! Yes!

I had to confess. The quicker the better. This ties in with the situation that obtained. She was no longer smiling but perusing my details on the computer and it was as if I had not existed, me personally: she had me conceptualized on a flat screen and was neglecting the very being that gave rise to the conceptualization.

I interrupted her when I spoke. But I had to. My memory is not great but it does work. I need to apologize, I said, because of last Tuesday.

She studied the screen as though I had not spoken.

I was trying hard to keep that appointment and I just failed. It was for a probable job of work and I want such a job, especially one that offers a pay. I need to clear off my debts and return to the fold. I require to get back on my feet and that job would have been ideal.

Now she replied: You gave me to understand that you would be here. I didnt expect you to let me down.

But I didnt let you down.

You didnt return.

Yes but I didnt let you down.

To not return is to let me down. For two days I kept this job alive. Others might have conceded but I thought it suitable for you, for you alone. The Office Manager spoke to me about it, she called me into Central Office. It was by way of a reprimand. I said you would be here and you were not.

She looked at me when she spoke. I found that difficult, and to distinguish her verbal utterances required a concentration beyond my own.

I was not used to being looked at. I dont want to be unfair to people of the female gender but this is my personal experience.

She was talking to me again. What in God's name was she saying? She was a forthright lady. Aged thirty-three. I knew she was. Thirty-three is an age I regard positively. She had a small face. Women I go for usually dont have small faces although I have got nothing against them, it is circumstances. But it may operate in reverse, that women who dont have small faces tend to be more interested in me. I am as putty in their hands. Women with small faces tend to go for other fellows, they go for obvious lookers. I am not an obvious looker. I would say for most women I am barely on the planet until if ever there comes a time, when that time arrives I shall be everywhere; look into my eyes and quiver ye lowly mortals. I shall have passed over but this is a form of transcendence and not a metaphorical reference to death man when I refer to death I make no bones and although I am being facetious that is truly what I believe, I hate all that fucking stuff; let us be honest between people, and more especially ones to whom we are attracted, and that includes male to male, I would never be exclusive about matters existentially crucial. It is what I am talking about.

She had finished and was waiting for me to respond. I nodded. What happened is I was actually robbed, I said. I had my bag, I said, it was the day after I left here. I was walking up by Roebuck Terrace and that little park they have there, they use it as an occasional music venue.

She frowned.

You dont like it there? I do. It is quiet; office workers and shop workers take in their sandwiches at lunchtime. Some feed the birds. They see the birds flying off into the blue sky and they have to return to the office. I was in the little park and I sat down on a bench, man I was tired, it was a while since I had slept. You know my circumstances. I think you do.

I waited for a comment. Instead she resumed from where she left off the last time.

That took me by surprise: I hadnt finished what I was going to say about how I hoisted up the old legs and fell asleep on that damn bench, so that is how the robbery took place, when I was asleep the dirty cowardly scoundrels: at least do the loathsome deed face to face etcetera etcetera. Except if the robber had been some poor bastard down on his luck, I suppose you could make a case for him. How was he to know I was in a bad way? in an even worse way than him. He would not have known. Why the hell didnt he ask! Especially if I was sleeping on a bench. Benches are not hotels. Then too the apparel, one tries to keep up but fashion tends to pass one fucking bye bye, the old catwalk and so on. Then if music is playing, music seems to play at important stages of my existence; at these times I am doing my utmost to concentrate on moments unconcerned with music, with non-musical moments, and there is a tension in this struggle, and this tension appears to impact psychologically. Normally I hear big extrovert symphonies. Schubert's Ninth. That is me, that is a day in my life. One actual day! It is like a whole world of human experience, it is just like goodness me!

Instead of me saying all that the bureaucrat woman stole the initiative and was doing the talking in her upper English accent. Maybe she was related to the Queen of Britain. Some of the Queen's relations are required to earn a crust in blue-chip defence ventures. She referred to important clients. On one's behalf a client was kept waiting for a period of three hours.

Who was this client?

She tapped the keyboard and I glimpsed a light flickering on my details, imprisoned forever. Certain phrases shimmered upward from the hard drive. I tried to read them before they vanished: clients are impressed by qualifications; promotional opportunities arise; salary scales are pleasing.

I shook my head in wonder. I was observed doing so. Would you be interested in less attractive options? she said, as though these existed. She did not wait for an answer but smiled remotely, tapping the keyboard and studying the screen. Here is one, she said. This is a provisional position. Opportunities for advancement

do not exist, which is normal practice. Do you understand that?

Yes, I said, where I come from we take early steps in
life.

Even should you indicate a willingness to learn and
improve your all-round workskills superiors will not
waive normal practice.

We dont begin with giant strides.

She stared at me. I smiled. I was not being sarcastic.
My language, however, was a challenge. People use language of this nature rarely. Not unless they themselves
are in an advantageous position. Advantageous.

When I left school I attended night classes and was
fortunate that one class featured the place of linguis-
tics in theories of economic psychology, being a grey
area loosely associated with traditional philosophy:
Celtic Continental as opposed to Roman. Roman
forms are by nature imperialistic, especially at the personal level where 'the negation of the other' is the key
to survival if not the ability to learn. The class was an
aid to intellectual life and this had a negative impact on
my capacity to serve and thereby earn a living in this
country where non-thinking automata have been the
vogue for for

For nothing. Since the dawn of the Holy Empire,
that deadening blanket of wrong reasoning, governed
governed and governed again.

I thought the bureaucrat woman intriguing and
hoped it was mutual. She gave me the address and interview card, advised me of the bus I could take to get to

this place of provisional employment. I stared at this card which was a pale green; lined, numbered and strongly luminal. I brought out my wallet, crushed the moths and blew off the dust, inserted the card into a compartment.

Then it was interview ended.

How had that happened? One minute I was sniffing her perfume the next I was stepping out onto the pavement.

Such is life. I am just so fucking trusting an individual. I always was. There is that bottom line with bureaucrats and some of the tools of their trade are tricks of deception. They get us doing things of which we, as it were, are unconscious. We seem to be unconscious. Yet we walk about and act in the world of other humans. It is not so much depressing as something less so, less depressing. I would have said it was not depressing, not at all, when I left the Agency on this occasion.

And it was this occasion and I was going to have to remember it was this occasion. And not forget.

She had diverted my attention. She had.

Here I was outside the actual building, and I had had plans.

I never leave buildings unless all internal possibility is sealed off. One wanders corridors. One has a look here and there. One makes discoveries. Too late now.

One's defences are there to be lowered. This problem is singular. It exists for all individuals. The bureaucrat woman and myself were of an age. I had reckoned on a kind of I dont know man honesty. From her.

Something. Is 'solidarity' too absurd a concept? Even using the word makes me turn my head a little, as though disguising my own naivety.

I shuffled along, then frowned and walked properly.

I felt like a think. There was a little grassy square with benches. I glanced to the sky then sat down.

One could only sigh.

Next thing I woke up! How long had I been sleeping! Who knows! No one. No one but God, and God is not a one, God is a all.

Still daylight. A bus; I spied it trundling round a far corner. On its near-side front window a sign read: 'World Freedom From Exhaust Day'. Until midnight all bus travel was free. What luck! I took the address and interview card out of my wallet, then flung away the wallet!

Why did I do that. The current proceedings, they induced in me trauma, the nature of luck and divine providence.

I read the address. Yes. This bus was mine! I would 'take it'. I would *take* this bus! Schubert's Ninth. I would visit my future workplace.

There was no necessity of doing this but with time to kill and no money to do it why not make use of the free travel? Woa me hearties. I broke into a trot as the bus hove to.

Travel allows the chance to think, to think to think to think; consult with oneself. I relished the prospect.

The driver was a hopeless rascal, I should have known: a fellow of my age, and with someone else's beard, not so much Lenin as that elderly chap with the full head of the stuff, Morris or Kropotkin, Bakunin. One presumes characters such as he hold revolutionary-grounded politics similar to one's own. Whenever I board their bus I give a conspiratorial twitch of the head. But it never works man it just never fucking works. An authoritarian right-wing arsehole; that is what he was, somebody who would rather lick the boots of the bosses than join a comrade in acts of liberation. As soon as I boarded the fucking bus he wanted to kick me off. It was no misunderstanding. All I did was seek directions allied to matters temporal. I had a sandwich. There are people in this world who exist in a state of siege. They construct a moat round themselves and are continually raising the drawbridge. He was one of them. Why be a bus driver if one refuses to answer questions concerning time and place? These should be matters of fact, not issues for debate.

One seethes.

Later I alighted. I located the place of provisional employment although it appeared deserted. It was an unprepossessing building altogether. I could not imagine being tethered within such a structure.

Nearby was a building site. It wasnt a massive operation but big enough for its own purposes. This would have suited me. Guys were strolling around with lengths of wood and assorted tools. Building sites were out in the open, unlike factories; desperate places wherein we humans might perish forever. I had been employed in the building industry before. Much the better option.

Perhaps there were vacancies. I could cross over the road to ascertain the likelihood. I was about to do this but recognized it as a psychological manoeuvre. Yet again I was trying to escape the true path. There was a path, why avoid it. Such was the mark of the coward. No, I would not run away. I would remain. I would confront the dark forces, perhaps foment a situation, take part in an epoch-changing strike.

The entrance gate into the parking area of the unprepossessing building lay ahead. Inside was a trailer but not much else. There were warning signs on Trespassing and Security. Suddenly a uniformed male appeared with a cup of tea or coffee in hand, a newspaper beneath his elbow, he yawned and spat to the ground. He had not seen me yet directed the spit towards the space into which I headed.

That boded ill. It meant he knew I was there. Probably he saw me from the trailer window and here he was keeping me at bay. I was tempted to return to the inner city. Mid to late afternoon. I would need a place soon. There was a cinema whose early evening entertainments provided a panacea for parties exhausted by life's travels. Persons dotted themselves about the hall and might sleep. Management's attitude was benign. When the programme ended the ushers roused individuals in a tentative – not to say sympathetic – manner. On one occasion one such usher panicked when unable to rouse me. I apologized for snoring. The usher apologized for wakening me. She had feared the worst, an inference drawn from the manner in which my head lolled. That to me was appalling. A lolling head at my time of life. I was a mere boy. (Sometimes I dreamed I was a man.)

But you needed money for the cinema. During mid-evenings I had access to a secret hidey-hole but a snag existed therein. I had to not-snore. This hidey-hole though secret lay within earshot of 'the existent other'.

Immediacy. Needs and necessity.

Meanwhile the uniformed male security stared in my direction. He knew I was there. I had a sandwich in my pocket. I could eat it while pondering a course of action.

A brainwave. What if I hoofed it back to the Agency? The bureaucrat woman probably worked until very late. I could invent a pretext to reenter the building and see her, then be dismissed by her. But this time I would concentrate very hard and not discover myself having exited the building. I would find a secure wee spot and bed down for the night. I didnt even need to see her, I could just secret my way into the building, maybe find a spare settee someplace.

Ah but this was the stuff of fantasy. I recognized it for the hollow ruse it was. I was about to lose myself in the subterranean depth of the subconscious. I had embarked on a shifty stratagem that would result in the bureaucrat woman mentioning her spare settee, that I might bunk there for the night and snuggle into her and be as one, we two, and raising myself onto my elbows, her below me, her eyes

*

It is amazing what our brains get up to.

I had no foolish dreams about sharing her bed. It didnt matter how presentable I was in my individual underwear pack. No point being silly about it. Such women have suitors. She could have been married. Probably to a Duke of England. I had noticed a number of 'high-quality' cars parked in the vicinity of the Agency. All had metallic fashion accessories, heraldic designs as befitting the class of vulture. What are these designs called again? I always forget. Perhaps her aristocrat suitor drove one such ... car. One hesitates to call them 'car'. He would have a sentry employee watching the door who would have recognized 'the prowler'. Me. I was the prowler. A 'high-velocity' rifle would be trained on my very skull. If I made the wrong move my brains would be blown away by the male security. And the powers-that-be would defend him to the very marlow, this being a society structured on sinecurial wealth and the veracity of inherited inequality.

But what if the bureaucrat woman was away home? Perhaps she had a husband and weans to feed? Perhaps she languished in spinster's quarters, bemoaning her lack of a man, and that man might be me.

There was an ATM across the road from the Agency. I could stand near there and watch for an opportunity to enter the premises. But what if a domestic security appeared? He might assume a 'high-level' burglary was in operation, that I was standing guard for a gang of bank robbers, then below street level and burrowing their way down to the vaulted dungeon wherein lie riches beyond one's wildest dreams. Gold bars and stocks of bullion. It would be better walking apace than standing guard. But even that reeks of suspicious behaviour and the domestic security would seek answers to awkward questions.

What to do? The rain the rain.

Goodness me the fucking rain!

I was standing outside the entrance gate to the carpark of the unprepossessing building and had yet to approach a decision, my brains a complete mess, and the rain! a fucking downpour. Not just rain! This was more than rain! Them big heavy dropulet gobs of that what do you call it when you are running for cover – water water all is water, water water where do you run? I hurried back and forth but found no place. I was fucking drenched to the skin. A matter of moments, that was all it took! I shrieked at the sky but to no avail. That huffy feeling came over me: why hasnt God presented me with a convenient doorway?

Inside the carpark I saw the light in the security trailer. Perhaps this was a benign intervention. I pushed open the gate. The rain beat down on me as I splashed through the puddles. Another sign read

WARNING KILLER DOGS OUT THE BACK

I stepped up to the trailer door, about to chap it, but I didnt. The uniformed male security would have been waiting there, concealed behind the door. He had seen me and would have watched my approach. But ye Heavens the weather! The rain maintained volume, pattering off the tin walls and ceiling. I needed shelter man no two-ways about it. I chapped thrice. He answered immediately but did not stand aside that I might enter the trailer. His hand hovered above the butt of his gun. He carried himself erect, shoulders stiffly back. This was to warn me that he could handle himself in an emergency. I had a sandwich in my pocket. Maybe I could feed him the fucking thing. I should say he was about sixty or something like that, seventy. My father was fifty-three the last I saw him, five fucking years ago though why I refer to him I dont know except, well, I was not about to have a physical scrap, not with a gun-totin stranger, elderly or not, especially one who reminded me of my so-to-speak daddy.

He gazed sideways and down over my head, seeking accomplices after the fact. I stayed silent. Now he waited. Eventually I gestured at the unprepossessing building, and realized the place was deserted. And that the rain had stopped, it had. Pools of water lay on the ground. It was no figment. His attitude had tempered. Something about his shoulders, a weariness.

Who sent you? he said.

I was wondering that myself but made no reply. I think I must have smiled slightly.